THE STORMS O...

The Duke of Wyden... Races is confident th... ...orses will be winners at the... ... instead of staying with the Duke ... ...ond, he has accepted an invitation from the Marchioness of Berkhampton.

He is astonished when, as he nears the house, he sees a young girl blocking the way. When he speaks to her he discovers she is mad, with a hideously disfiguring face, and defiantly tells him that is how she will look when he attempts to marry her.

He assures Aldora he has no intention of marrying anyone but she tells him that her mother is determined she will be his wife and she hates him.

The Duke decides she is mentally deranged but when he reaches the house he finds the Marchioness and Queen Victoria are offering him the most important post in the British Empire if he consents to the marriage.

How he is forced to pursue Aldora who runs away – how they encounter danger and how the Duke finally weathers the storm is told in this 346th book by Barbara Cartland.

OTHER BOOKS BY BARBARA CARTLAND

Romantic Novels, over 350, the most recently published being:

A Miracle in Music
A Marriage Made in Heaven
Light from the Gods
From Hate to Love
Love on the Wind
The Duke Comes Home
Journey to a Star
Love and Lucia
The Unwanted Wedding
Gypsy Magic

Help from the Heart
A Duke in Danger
Lights, Laughter and a Lady
The Unbreakable Spell
Diona and a Dalmatian
Fire in the Blood
The Scots Never Forget
The Rebel Princess
A Witch's Spell
Secrets

The Dream and the Glory
(in aid of the St. John Ambulance Brigade)

Autobiographical and Biographical

The Isthmus Years 1919–1939
The Years of Opportunity 1939–1945
I Search for Rainbows 1945–1976
We Danced All Night 1919–1929
Ronald Cartland (with a Foreword by Sir Winston Churchill)
Polly My Wonderful Mother
I Seek the Miraculous

Historical:

Bewitching Women
The Outrageous Queen (The story of Queen Christina of Sweden)
The Scandalous Life of King Carol
The Private Life of Elizabeth, Empress of Austria
Josephine, Empress of France
Diane de Poitiers
Metternich – the Passionate Diplomat

Sociology:

You in the Home	Etiquette
The Fascinating Forties	The Many Facets of Love
Marriage for Moderns	Sex and the Teenager
Be Vivid, Be Vital	The Book of Charm
Love, Life and Sex	Living Together
Vitamins for Vitality	The Youth Secret
Husbands and Wives	The Magic of Honey
Men are Wonderful	Book of Beauty & Health

Keep Young and Beautiful by Barbara Cartland and Elinor Glyn.

Cookery:

Barbara Cartland's Health Food Cookery Book
Food for Love
Magic of Honey Cookbook
Recipes for Lovers

Editor of:

The Common Problems by Ronald Cartland (with a preface by the Rt. Hon. the Earl of Selborne, P.C.)
Barbara Cartland's Library of Love
Barbara Cartland's Library of Ancient Wisdom
'Written with Love' Passionate love letters selected by Barbara Cartland

Drama:

Blood Money
French Dressing

Philosophy:

Touch the Stars

Radio Operetta:

The Rose and the Violet (Music by Mark Lubbock) performed in 1942.

Radio Plays:

The Caged Bird: An episode in the Life of Elizabeth Empress of Austria. Performed in 1957.

General:

Barbara Cartland's Book of Useless Information, with a Foreword by The Earl Mountbatten of Burma. (In aid of the United Colleges)
Love and Lovers (Picture Book)
The Light of Love (Prayer Book)
Barbara Cartland's Scrapbook (in Aid of the Royal Photographic Museum)
Romantic Royal Marriages
Barbara Cartland's Book of Celebrities

Verse:

Lines of Life and Love

Music

An Album of Love Songs sung with the Royal Philharmonic Orchestra.

Film

The Flame is Love

Cartoons:

Barbara Cartland Romances (Book of Cartoons) has recently been published in the U.S.A. and Great Britain and in other parts of the world.

THE STORMS OF LOVE

BARBARA CARTLAND

CORGI BOOKS

THE STORMS OF LOVE
A CORGI BOOK 0 552 12446 X

First publication in Great Britain

PRINTING HISTORY
Corgi edition published 1985

Copyright © Barbara Cartland 1985

Corgi Books are published by Transworld Publishers Ltd., Century House, 61–63 Uxbridge Road, Ealing, London W5 5SA, in Australia by Transworld Publishers (Aust.) Pty. Ltd., 26 Harley Crescent, Condell Park, NSW 2200, and in New Zealand by Transworld Publishers (N.Z.) Ltd., Cnr. Moselle and Waipareira Avenues, Henderson, Auckland.

Printed and bound in Great Britain by
Cox & Wyman Ltd., Reading, Berks.

ABOUT THE AUTHOR

Barbara Cartland, the world's most famous romantic novelist, who is also an historian, playwright, lecturer, political speaker and television personality, has now written over 350 books and sold over 350 million books over the world.

She has also had many historical works published and has written four autobiographies as well as the biographies of her mother and that of her brother, Ronald Cartland, who was the first Member of Parliament to be killed in the last war. This book has a preface by Sir Winston Churchill and has just been republished with an introduction by Sir Arthur Bryant.

"Love at the Helm" a novel written with the help and inspiration of the late Earl Mountbatten of Burma, Uncle of His Royal Highness Prince Philip, is being sold for the Mountbatten Memorial Trust.

Miss Cartland in 1978 sang an Album of Love Songs with the Royal Philharmonic Orchestra.

In 1976 by writing twenty-one books, she broke the world record and has continued for the following six years with 24, 20, 23, 24, 24 and 25. In the Guinness Book of Records she is listed as the world's top-selling author.

In private life Barbara Cartland, who is a Dame of Grace of the Order of St. John of Jerusalem, Chairman of the St. John Council in Hertfordshire and Deputy President of the St. John Ambulance Brigade, has fought for better conditions and salaries for Midwives and Nurses.

She has championed the cause for old people, had the law altered regarding gypsies and founded the first Romany Gypsy camp in the world.

Barbara Cartland is deeply interested in Vitamin therapy, and is President of the National Association for Health.

Her designs "Decorating with Love" are being sold all over the U.S.A. and the National Home Fashions League made her, in 1981, "Woman of Achievement".

Barbara Cartland's Romances (Book of Cartoons) has been published in Great Britain, and the U.S.A.

AUTHOR'S NOTE

The Russian infiltration into Afghanistan in 1873 was a mistake on the part of the Viceroy of India, Lord Northbrook and the Gladstone Government in England.

Afghanistan, the wild, mountainous, independent Moslem country to the North of India was governed by the Amir Sher Ali after a bloody struggle for the succession.

Sher Ali had no wish to be beholden to either the British or the Russians, but as the former crept even closer to his Northern borders he was wise enough to know he would have to seek the protection of one or other of them.

He feared the Russians more than the British and he therefore sent a special envoy to the Viceroy, Lord Northbrook in 1873 offering a treaty which in return for his allegiance to the British would guarantee him an annual subsidy and recognise his youngest son Abdulla Jan as his heir.

Lord Northbrook, a dry stick of a man, colourless and unimaginative, more interested in statistics than people, was instructed by Mr. Gladstone and the Prime Minister had not only to refuse the office but to "tick off" Sher Ali for the imprisonment of his eldest and rebellious son Yakah Khan.

Offended and angry Sher Ali turned to Russia and there was no doubt that Lord Northbrook's action was responsible for the endless conflict with Afghanistan, stirred up by the Russians, which followed.

Today we cannot help wondering if the Russian influence in 1878 and their provocation thereafter with Afghanistan, might in some way have influenced their decision and in 1981 to over-ride and conquer it.

Historically Lord Northbrook who resigned as Viceroy

of India in 1875 was succeeded by Lord Lytton. He was unambitious, unconventional, a dreamer and a romantic poet.

He was faced with one trial after another – the most famous of the century, the Second Afghan War, massacre and financial disaster. But his handling of the famine brought permanent advantages to India and his foresight strengthened Disraeli's Afghan policy and made it workable. Through every difficulty he never lost the support and sympathy of Queen Victoria.

CHAPTER ONE

1875

Driving to the Goodwood Races the Duke of Wydeminster thought with satisfaction that his team of horses was the most outstanding that he had ever owned.

Once again, he told himself, he had been proved right, having bought them as foals at a sale held by one of his friends, when the majority of buyers had not considered them worth a second glance.

The Duke however with his expert eye had sensed the possibilities in them, and they were now the envy of everybody who saw them.

He looked forward to the congratulations he would receive when he reached the Races not only from the Duke of Richmond but from the other leading owners who would undoubtedly be present.

Goodwood, the Duke was thinking, was not only the most beautiful Race-Course in England, but one of the most enjoyable.

Set overlooking the wide lush green coastal plain from which one could see with the naked eye the English Channel, the Isle of Wight, and Chichester Cathedral, it was unique with its breath-taking view over the Downs.

It was also, which was something the Duke particularly enjoyed, redolent with history.

Whenever he went to Goodwood he found himself thinking of it romantic origin, the first Duke of Richmond having been the son of Charles II and the 'Fair Maid of France', Louise de Kérouaille.

Unlike some of the King's other Mistresses who were of

low birth, Louise, a Breton was the daughter of a French nobleman and was Lady-in-Waiting to Charles's favourite sister, the Duchess of Orleans.

It was always said that Charles's love for Louise was different from the love he had for any of his other mistresses, and in 1673 he created her Duchess of Portsmouth.

From that time until the end of the King's reign twelve years later she exercised a special influence over him and undoubtedly affected the nation's relationship with France.

Her son by the King was three years old when he was given the titles of Duke of Richmond, Earl of March, and Baron Settrington.

But the Duke of Wydeminster was thinking more of Charles II, to whom he often thought that in many ways, although not particularly in appearance, he had a close resemblance.

Certainly Charles II had excelled in sports, as he did and was vitally concerned with the development and prudent management of the nation, as the Duke was with his vast estates.

What was more, they undoubtedly had a close affinity in their appreciation of female beauty, although regrettably neither the King's nor the Duke's affairs lasted very long.

At the same time, the Duke thought to himself, women made life very enjoyable.

He was looking ahead now with almost a feeling of excitement to the Beauty who he knew would be waiting for him when he arrived at Berkhampton House.

It was a departure from the usual that he was not staying at Goodwood with the Duke.

He had of course, received His Grace's invitation with the assumption that he would be the principal guest in Goodwood House and on the Race-Course.

But the Duke had at the same time, received a pressing note from the Marchioness of Berkhampton begging him to honour her by his presence.

He was just about to refuse when he realised that Lady Newbury would also be a guest of the Marchioness.

Fenella Newbury had attracted his eye from the first moment he had seen her at a Ball.

He had thought her one of the most beautiful women he had seen for a long time, but he had not paid her a great deal of attention because her husband, Lord Newbury, was not one of the close circle of his special friends.

When, however, unexpectedly he sat next to her at dinner the following week as the guest of one of the Ambassadors at the Court of St. James, he found that she was lovelier than he remembered.

Also the moment she looked at him there was an expression in her eyes that told the Duke that like most women he met she was overwhelmed by his appearance and very receptive to his attractions.

The Duke would have been a fool, and he was in fact, a very clever man, if he had not known that he had a special magnetism that drew women to him as if he was the Pied Piper.

It was something one could not put into words, but it was nevertheless what he often thought to himself was a gift from the gods.

It had certainly made his life a pleasant, scented bed of roses.

At the same time, he was honest enough to realise that it had its distractions as well as its advantages.

It meant that like the King with whom he identified himself no women lasted long in his life and he was invariably the one to become bored first.

In fact he had never known a woman at any time, to be bored with him, and he often wondered why he had the power to make them so wildly, overwhelmingly in love that they invariably lost not only their hearts, but their heads.

The Duke was not a cruel man, in fact he was extremely

compassionate, especially to animals and those in straitened circumstances.

His generosity was well-known, and he was cheered so long and loudly on every Race Course not only because his horses won – and the English have always loved a sportsman – but also because of his innumerable acts of kindness.

His generosity in the sporting world and to everybody who appealed to him for help had gradually become known to the Public and they appreciated him for that as well as for everything else.

Where his women were concerned however, he was forced to leave them weeping, and to know that although he had had no intention of doing so, he had broken their hearts.

It seemed inevitable that what started as a light-hearted and amusing *affaire de coeur*, a game between two sophisticated, experienced people, eventually became a battle-field with a victim left wounded but that was never the Duke.

As he had said to his confidential secretary, who ran his household and knew all the ups and down of his personal life:

"It is ridiculous that I cannot dispense with my mistresses without a scene that would seem overdramatic at Drury Lane."

He was, at that moment, not speaking of an affair in the Social World, but with a pretty ballerina whom he had installed in a house in St. John's Wood, but with whom he had finished because she no longer attracted him.

According to the rules, when a Protector abdicated and paid handsomely for the pleasure he had enjoyed, there should be no tears, no recriminations, while the 'Cyprian' in question went back into circulation very much richer, and usually with some valuable trophies to show for the experience.

But where the Duke was concerned, there were clinging arms, steaming eyes, and wailing voices pleading with him to stay and asking over and over again what had gone wrong.

"It is not exactly that there is anything wrong," he mused, "it is just that sooner or later an uneducated woman, however talented, however pretty, fails to interest me."

That seemed reasonable enough until he thought of his conquests in the Social World, of whom he might almost say the same.

It was true that the ladies in question were better educated, some even had a sparkling wit, and could certainly discuss the political situation or the latest scandal in high places as her lowlier sister was unable to do.

But that invariably, the Duke found, led to her discussing him and his relationship with her, so that the conversation always got back to the same starting-place, which was the passion they aroused in each other, and which involved only their bodies and not their brains.

Mr. Greyshot, his secretary, knew that the Duke did not expect an answer to his question, but for once he decided to give him one and he replied:

"I think, Your Grace, the whole trouble is, if you will forgive me saying so, you are spoilt!"

"Spoilt?" the Duke ejaculated and the word rang out like a pistol-shot.

"My mother used to tell me when I was a boy to count my blessings," Mr. Greyshot said, "and when I count yours, as I frequently have to do, I find it makes a very long list and an incredibly satisfactory one!"

The Duke smiled.

"I agree with you, Greyshot, and I am not ungrateful to the fates, or to the Almighty, whichever you prefer. I was, in fact, thinking as you are aware, not of my possessions, but of the women in my life."

"All the same, Your Grace," Mr. Greyshot persisted, "you have an attraction for the 'Fair Sex' which they find irresistible, and in consequence they wish to hold onto you and it is agonising for them to be forced to let you go."

"As I know to my cost," the Duke said beneath his breath.

"There is another adage which I think applies in this instance," Mr. Greyshot continued, "which is 'nothing is for free', one pays for everything one receives."

"You can hardly accuse me of not settling my debts," the Duke said sharply.

"I was not speaking of cash, Your Grace."

"I am aware of that, at the same time it is usually an efficacious salve to a bleeding heart."

"Not where Your Grace is concerned."

His secretary spoke quietly and with a sincerity that was unmistakable.

For a moment the Duke glared at him. Then he laughed.

"All right, Greyshot, you win!" he said. "But what you are implying makes me feel very conceited."

Thinking over the conversation the Duke thought now that he certainly had a lot to be conceited about, and added to his long list of conquests by the end of Goodwood Races would undoubtedly be Fenella Newbury.

Thinking of her because she was so lovely, the Duke felt a sudden quickening in the part of his anatomy where he thought he kept his heart.

Although he was unaware of it, there was a sparkle in his eyes in anticipation of what lay ahead.

It was the same feeling, he thought, that he experienced at the end of a stalk when he put his rifle to his shoulder and drew a bead on what was known as 'The King of the Moors' silhouetted against the purple heather.

He felt it when riding in the front of the field with the hounds just behind the fox, and it was only a question of seconds before they over-ran him.

He felt it when he brought down a high pheasant that to any other gun was out of reach, and there was now that same excitement within his breast and a satisfaction which would make any man feel conceited.

"I suppose in some ways I am exceptional," he ruminated as he drove on, "just as Charles II was exceptional in his way, and we both of us manage to make the world a merrier place because we are in it."

He smiled at the idea and wondered if Fenella Newbury was waiting impatiently for his arrival and feeling as he was.

It was astute of the Marchioness of Berkhampton, he thought, to have held Fenella out as a bait to induce him to be her guest rather than to stay as he usually did at Goodwood House.

West Sussex was thick with noble mansions, and their noble owners all competed with each other to fill their houses with the most important and the most amusing members of Society for Goodwood Week.

West Dean, Stansted, Uppark, Cowdray, Petworth and Arundel were packed with the most distinguished names in the land.

They would converge on them with valets, lady's-maids, coaches, Phaetons, Victorias and Broughams, besides of course grooms and horses to fill every stable to overflowing.

Many of the distinguished guests were racehorse owners but none could boast better blood-stock than the Duke of Wydeminster.

With another feeling of satisfaction he was quite certain that his horses would carry off at least three or four of the most coveted trophies of the meeting.

The Duke of Richmond, he knew, would be a formidable rival, for the Duke was a great expert on horse-flesh and had himself, as the Earl of March, ridden five winners at the Goodwood Races of 1842.

'He may be hurt that I am not staying with him,' the Duke thought, 'but I dare say he will guess the reason when he sees me with Fenella.'

He was well aware that it was almost impossible for him to hide his love-affairs from the inquisitive world in which he moved.

He often thought they knew who he was making love to before it actually happened.

But that was the penalty of importance and of being a bachelor.

At least he did not have to worry, he reflected, about a jealous wife or, what could be much more irksome, 'keeping up appearances in public.'

He anticipated he would have no trouble with Lord Newbury, although some of his charmers' husbands had been inclined to become aggressive.

He had, in fact, fought three duels and, most unjustly, he had in each case been the winner of the contest.

"I suppose if there was any justice in life," the Duke had once said to Mr. Greyshot, "I should have my arm in a sling today rather than poor Underwood who had definitely every reason to be aggrieved at my behaviour!"

Mr. Greyshot had laughed.

"I thought Lord Underwood was very brave in challenging Your Grace," he said. "Most husbands are learning to turn a blind eye when you are about, as they do not like being made to look a fool."

As it happened the Duke often felt rather sorry for them.

He told himself that if he ever married, which he had no intention of doing for a great many years, he would never allow himself to be in the position of a cuckolded husband.

It would be 'poetic justice' he thought, but knew confidently that it never would happen.

He was now getting near to Goodwood and there was a touch of sea-salt in the air.

Everywhere he looked there was that particular beauty that he associated with this part of England, and which in consequence he enjoyed more and more everytime he came here.

He found himself almost envying the Duke of Richmond that his estate was situated in this part of the country.

Then he knew it would be very hard for anything to equal the magnificence of Wyde, his family house in Buckinghamshire.

From it there was a magnificent view, and against its background of woods it glowed like a jewel – a very large and precious jewel – at which everybody seeing it for the first time, gasped in sheer amazement.

Thinking of his home made the Duke remember that only a week ago – when he had entertained a house-party there – his grandmother had acted as hostess.

Once a great beauty, she was still at seventy an extremely impressive and lovely-looking woman.

But she had a sharp tongue and never hesitated to express her opinions with a forthrightness which many people found intimidating.

She had taken her grandson to task as nobody else would have dared to do and informed him bluntly that it was time he settled down and took a wife.

"You need not try to bully me, Grandmama," the Duke said. "I have no intention of being married until I am too old to enjoy myself as I do now, and that will be when I have one foot in the grave!"

"You have to have an heir!" the Dowager had snapped.

"Of course," the Duke agreed, "and I shall make sure, as my father omitted to do, that I do not have one son, but several."

He knew this was a slightly unsporting reply, in fact what was known as 'hitting below the belt', for it had been a great disappointment to his grandmother that her only son, the Duke's father, had also produced only him and not a number of brothers to make sure of the succession.

"Then my advice is to get on with it!" The Duchess said quite unabashed.

"I understand your feelings, Grandmama, but I am more concerned with my own."

"A wife need not interfere very noticeably with your pleasures," the Dowager said reflectively. "You would always behave with propriety towards her, and doubtless the poor thing will fall head-over-heels in love with you, as all those other foolish women contrive to do!"

The Duke laughed.

"You are not very complimentary, Grandmama!"

"Oh, I know you fancy yourself," the Duchess said, "strutting about like a peacock with a dozen little peahens scurrying after you! But I want to hold your son in my arms before I die!"

"That gives me at least twenty years!" the Duke remarked. "Our families are renowned for their longevity."

"Compliments will not prevent me from telling you that you are wasting your time, your energy and your brains!" the Duchess said firmly.

"It is a matter of opinion. My time is my own, and so is my energy," the Duke replied. "As for my brain, I devote quite a lot of it to the Bills which come before the House of Lords, and although you may not wish to believe it, the Prime Minister often asks my advice."

"I should hope so!" the Duchess replied. "At the same time, you should be setting up a family and thinking of the future rather than over-indulging in the present!"

The Duke laughed again.

"When I find a young woman who will grace the position that you held, and wear the family jewels as you did, then I will certainly consider asking her to be my wife."

"A very elusive reply!" the Duchess scoffed. "You know as well as I do that you never meet unmarried girls. In fact I was going to suggest I should bring two or three to the next party we have at Wyde for your inspection."

The Duke gave a cry of horror.

"I have never heard such a monstrous suggestion!" he exclaimed. "If you dare, Grandmama, to bring one unfledged chick through my front door, I shall leave immediately and you can entertain her on your own!"

His grandmother made a helpless, but graceful gesture of her hand.

"Very well, Ingram," she said, "go your own way, but I

warn you, you are letting down the whole family and ignoring the responsibility to which you were born."

"Nonsense!" the Duke said firmly.

He had kissed her cheek, but when he left her the Duchess sat with a worried expression in her old eyes.

She was wondering how she could convince him that to provide a son to inherit the Kingdom over which he ruled was an urgent necessity.

The Duke, as he had told his grandmother, had no intention of marrying.

Why should he saddle himself with a wife who would doubtless be a bore from the very moment he was married to her, and unlike the other women who bored him could not be paid off and dispensed with.

He could image the horror of listening to the same banal remarks at breakfast, luncheon, tea and dinner for the next thirty or forty years.

He could imagine how frustrating it would be to have to disguise his love-affairs a great deal more skilfully than he had to do at the moment.

A wife would also certainly put paid to the very amusing parties he gave at Wyde to which his grandmother was not invited.

And the even better ones which he gave in London and to which his men-friends looked forward eagerly and were constantly pressing him to have another.

'No, a wife would definitely be an encumbrance and a headache that I refuse to inflict upon myself,' the Duke thought firmly.

Then once again he was thinking of Fenella and the obvious invitation in her eyes that would welcome him when he arrived at Berkhampton House.

He was almost prepared to wager too that Lord Newbury who was very much older than his wife and was not really interested in racing, would not be present.

He preferred shooting, and the Duke had already made a

mental note that he should invite him to the shoots at Wyde, accompanied of course, by the delectable Fenella.

It might not be so easy to have her alone on these occasions, but he was a past-master at finding an excuse for taking the woman in whom he was interested, round the Picture Gallery alone, or when the weather was fine, showing her the view from the roof.

Better still, he would find a convenient moment to visit her when she was resting in her *Boudoir* while the men were all playing cards or billiards before dinner.

Then after the shooting season, the Duke thought, there would be the Hunt Ball – but that was planning too far ahead.

He suddenly had the uncomfortable feeling, which he quickly dismissed from his mind, that by that time Fenella's place might have been taken by somebody else!

It was not quite five o'clock when the Duke turned his horses in through the fine and impressive gates of Berkhampton House.

The third Marquis of Berkhampton had died some years ago and as the present Marquis was still at Eton, he was not likely to be playing host at the party taking place in his house for the Races.

But the Duke, who had frequently been a guest of the Marchioness in London, knew she was a most efficient hostess.

Immensely rich, the Berkhamptons entertained on a very grand scale, and before the Prince Consort's death in 1861 the Queen was a frequent visitor and a close friend of the Marchioness.

The Marchioness was in fact, not only an Hereditary Lady of the Bed-Chamber, but a personage at Court who was admired and respected not only by the Courtiers, but by Ambassadors and representatives of every foreign country who visited England.

In fact, it was said that they were always jokingly advised: 'Make yourself pleasant to the Queen, but whatever happens keep in with the Marchioness of Berkhampton!'

The Duke found her witty and amusing, and enjoyed being in her company.

He was sure he would have no regrets in having turned down Goodwood House, and as he passed through the gates he thought once again that he was definitely going to enjoy himself.

There was a mile long drive bordered by ancient oak-trees and the horses were moving along it at a good pace when suddenly the Duke saw ahead somebody standing in the way.

As he drew nearer he expected whoever it was to step to one side.

Then he saw to his surprise that there was a barrier of branches from the trees lying across the drive and in the centre of them there was a woman.

He brought his horses to a standstill expecting the woman to come and tell him why the road was blocked, but she did not move.

After a moment he said to his groom who was seated beside him:

"Find out what is wrong, Jim, or clear the path!"

There was a slight hesitation before the groom replied:

"I thinks, Your Grace, that be a young lady standing there!"

The Duke looked a little more closely and saw that his groom was right.

What he had thought to be a woman from the village, placed there to inform passers-by that they had to make a diversion, was in fact a woman dressed in a gown with a small bustle, which was obviously a dress that would have been worn only by a Lady.

The woman made no effort to move, but waited and because the Duke thought it was undignified to shout he handed his reins to his groom, and stepping down from his Phaeton walked towards the figure in the centre of the road.

He wondered as he did so, if it was perhaps some childish prank or a joke being played on him by one of the more obstreperous members of the house-party.

Then as he reached the woman who had still not moved he saw to his astonishment that she had the figure of a slim young girl, but she was making the most hideous face he had ever seen in his whole life.

Her eyes were turned inward so that they crossed and with the fingers of both hands she had contorted her mouth so that it was grotesque, like that of a clown, stretching across her face almost from ear to ear.

He stood looking at her and as she did not move he could not be certain because her eyes were crossed whether she was looking at him or not.

"What is this all about?" he asked. "As you must be aware, I wish to reach the house."

There was a little pause. Then the girl, without taking her fingers from the corners of her mouth said in a somewhat constricted voice:

"Look at me! I want you to look at me!"

"I am looking," the Duke replied grimly, "But it is not a pleasant sight!"

"Good!"

As she spoke the girl took her fingers from her mouth her eyes went back into place and she said, looking up at him:

"Did you see how ugly I looked?"

"Of course I saw!" the Duke replied, "and may I say if it is a joke I do not consider it very funny!"

"It was not meant to be funny," the girl replied. "I wanted you to feel appalled, and if possible disgusted, that any woman could look so ugly, so revolting!"

"All right, I agree," the Duke said. "Now if you are satisfied I would like to proceed on my way and perhaps you will allow my man to remove the obstruction from the drive."

He looked down as he spoke and saw that what had seemed from a distance a formidable barrier was in fact, only a few light pieces of fallen wood and boughs with leaves on them.

"He can do that," the girl replied, "but first I want to speak to you."

"What about?" the Duke asked in a slightly hostile manner.

"It will not take long, and if you will just come out of ear-shot of your groom there is a tree-trunk on which we can sit."

The Duke was surprised. At the same time he thought it would be difficult to refuse point-blank to talk to this young woman.

At any rate it was impossible to drive on without the rubbish, which he suspected she had put there, being cleared.

After a moment's hesitation he said:

"I cannot imagine what this is all about, but if it pleases you, I will listen to what you have to say."

Almost before he had finished speaking she started to walk over the grass passing between two of the oaks to where the Duke saw as he followed her, there lay the trunk of a fallen tree.

He wondered what she could possibly have to say to him and only hoped whatever it might be that it would not take long.

Now that he had reached Berkhampton House he was anxious to go inside.

He also felt thirsty after the dust of the road, which because there had been no rain for sometime, was excessive.

The girl, having reached the tree-trunk sat down, and the Duke now realised he had at first taken her for an employee on the estate because she wore no bonnet.

Instead her head was bare and the sunshine percolating through the branches of the trees above them made a pattern of gold on her head.

Looking at her it seemed extraordinary that she had managed to contort her face into anything so monstrously ugly as when he had first seen her.

He saw now that her features were delicate and while she was not strictly beautiful, she was, he thought, somewhat unusual.

Her grey eyes seemed enormous in her pointed face, and despite the gold of her hair, her eye-lashes were dark at the roots and curling upwards were fair at the tips.

He saw that she was looking at him somewhat apprehensively, and as he sat down gingerly on the tree-trunk beside her, hoping the bark would not mar the perfection of his close-fitting drain-pipe trousers, he said:

"What is troubling you? If you are a guest of the Marchioness surely what you have to say could have waited until my arrival?"

"No, I will not have a chance to speak to you then," the girl replied, "and it is absolutely imperative that you listen to me now."

"Very well," the Duke answered. "I am listening, but as you obviously know who I am, perhaps we might start by my knowing your name."

"I am Aldora Hampton!"

The Duke looked at her in surprise before he said slowly:

"You are one of the Marchioness's daughters?"

"I am the youngest and the only one who is not *married.*"

She accentuated the last word and as the Duke looked at her speculatively she said quickly:

"Now listen, because we have not much time. Mama is determined that you shall marry me, and if you have any sense you will turn round and leave immediately!"

For a moment the Duke found it hard to express himself.

Then he gave a light laugh before he said:

"I assure you, Lady Aldora, you need not be disturbed on my behalf, if that is what troubles you, for I have no intention of marrying anybody!"

"And I have no intention of marrying you!" Lady Aldora replied. "But it is what Mama intends and she invariably gets here own way."

"In this case she will be disappointed," the Duke said, "but I think you must be mistaken, and your mother has no such intention."

He was thinking as he spoke that if the Marchioness had in fact considered him as a prospective husband for her daughter, and it had never entered his mind that she might do so, she would then not have invited Fenella Newbury to this particular party.

"You do not understand," Aldora said, "and I suppose it is difficult for somebody who does not know Mama as well as I do, but I promise you your freedom is in danger!"

She paused and went on aggressively:

"If you agree to marry me I shall make myself look at the end of your table, exactly as I did just now, and you will not only be ashamed of me, but you will be the laughing-stock of all your friends!"

The Duke could hardly believe what he was hearing.

It flashed through his mind that the Marchioness's younger daughter was not quite right in the head.

Yet as he looked at the delicate face looking up into his and saw the clearness of her eyes, it was hard to think she was anything but normal.

"I know you are thinking I am mad," Aldora said before he could speak, "but I promise you that Mama intends that you shall be my husband."

"Has she told you so?" the Duke enquired.

"She has made it very clear that she admires you, and that you are the most important bachelor in the country! I think, although I cannot imagine how, that she will contrive to bring some sort of pressure to bear on you, so that you will find it impossible to refuse to do as she wishes."

The Duke could not think what this could be and he merely answered:

"That is nonsense! And let me make it very clear, Lady Aldora, that I have no wish to marry anybody, nor do I intend to do so!"

"I thought that was what you would say, and for my own part, I swear nothing would make me marry you!"

She spoke with such violence that the Duke was taken aback.

It was not the usual attitude of any woman towards him, and because he was curious he could not help asking:

"I accept of course, that you feel like that, at the same time I should be interested to know why you hold me in such revulsion?"

"Do you really think that I would want to marry a man who spends his life making love to other men's wives," Aldora asked, "and having sucked them dry, as if they were an orange throws them away and then looks round for another?"

The deliberate rudeness of what she said made the Duke feel his temper rising.

"There is no point in continuing this conversation," he said in an icy voice which invariably made anybody who listened to it shake at the knees.

He rose as he spoke, but Aldora clapped her hands with delight and exclaimed:

"Good! Now you are hating me. I can be abominable and, as I have shown you, very ugly. Promise me that you will tell Mama that you absolutely refuse to offer me marriage."

"You can rest assured of that," the Duke said coldly, "and I think, Lady Aldora, that this conversation, which is quite ridiculous, had best be forgotten."

"I think you will remember it," Aldora replied, "and

realise that I loathe everything about you. If you do ask me to marry you, I shall run away to France where nobody will ever find me again!"

It passed through the Duke's mind that was about the best thing she could do.

But he thought it ws beneath his dignity to bandy any more words with a girl who was obviously touched in the head and should not in consequence be allowed to marry anybody.

He started to walk back towards the Phaeton and jumping up from the tree-trunk Aldora followed him.

"Now stick to your guns," she instructed him, "and whatever Mama says to you, tell her that nothing would make you marry me. If ever I have to marry, it would not be to a man like you!"

This was a parting shot as the Duke was climbing into his Phaeton to take the reins from his groom.

As he did so, he could not help replying:

"When you find him, he has all my sympathy!"

He turned his head to say:

"Clear the road, Jim!"

As the groom hastily obeyed and started lifting the branches from the drive, Aldora went to the other side and began to do the same.

Then as the road was cleared and the Duke was able to move his horses forward she looked up at him and as he passed gave him an ironic, military salute.

As she did so, she smiled and it transformed her face in a way that made her look quite different from what she had before.

Her eyes seemed to sparkle and the Duke saw there were two dimples on either side of her mouth.

Then as Jim climbed up he drove on, thinking as he saw the big house ahead of him that the Marchioness had a blot on the family escutcheon of which few people could be aware.

"The girl to put it kindly, has bats in the belfry!" he told himself. "I expect she is kept under strict supervision and not allowed to mix in the ordinary way with the other guests."

The Duke drew his horses up to the front door and as he brought them to a standstill hoped this was true, and he would not have to encounter the rude, impertinent Lady Aldora again.

CHAPTER TWO

When the Duke came down to dinner he was looking forward to the evening with what was for him an unusual enthusiasm.

He had known when he was greeted by the Marchioness how pleased she was to see him, and she said in what he thought was a meaningful way:

"I have tried to arrange a party, my dear Ingram which you will find amusing."

She smiled and added with the charm for which she was famous:

"I am very honoured of course that you have come to stay with me instead of going to Goodwood House."

The Duke thought that he had made an excellent choice.

His bedroom was exceedingly comfortable, with a Sitting-Room attached to it, and was one of the best in the house.

He suspected, although he had not yet asked any questions, that Fenella Newbury would be near him. She would not be in a room that communicated with his Sitting-Room – that would be too obvious but he was sure she would be on the same landing, and perhaps on the opposite side of the corridor.

It was understood in all the great houses he visited, with a discretion that was never abused, that those who were indulging in *affaires de coeur* were put as conveniently near to each other as possible.

The Duke however asked no questions, not even who was in the house-party, but as she talked the Marchioness dropped first one name, then another.

This told him that quite a number of his personal friends were staying at Berkhampton House, as well as Fenella Newbury.

He had been aware for a long time that very little went on in the Social World in which the Marchioness was an undoubted leader, without her being aware of it.

Because she was still a very attractive woman he flirted with her skilfully, paid her compliments, and was aware, as he had known before, that he was one of the people at Court whom she favoured.

When he came down to dinner he had almost forgotten about his encounter with Lady Aldora, and had dismissed it as unimportant.

He was therefore surprised when he entered the Drawing-Room to see standing beside his hostess somebody in white who he realised was the extremely rude young woman who had accosted him in the drive.

As he walked towards the Marchioness, moving with a dignity that was habitual to him, he knew she was watching him appreciatively while the girl beside her had her eyes on the ground.

As the Duke reached the Marchioness's side she said:

"I think you know everybody here tonight, with the exception of my daughter Aldora."

The Duke inclined his head and Aldora curtsied with a grace he could not help noticing, though she still did not raise her eyes.

He was aware that she was extremely well-dressed in a very attractive gown of white gauze which made her seem somewhat insubstantial, and unlike her mother, who was blazing with diamonds, she wore only two white roses in her golden hair.

She looked young, demure, quite conventional.

Very different, the Duke thought, from the small virago who had insulted him and told him how much she hated

30

him in an offensive manner which he did not wish to remember.

Fortunately before there was any need to speak, a number of other guests came into the Drawing-Room.

Almost the first of them, the Duke saw, was the one he particularly wanted to see.

As she came through the door under the light from the chandeliers he knew she was even lovelier than he remembered.

Fenella Newbury at twenty-seven was at the height of her beauty.

Tall, exquisitely curved, and dressed in a manner which made the very most of her figure, she had fair hair that deepened to russet brown.

Her eyes however were the vivid blue of a summer sky, her complexion was clear, and her skin very white against a gown that echoed the colour of her eyes.

Like the Marchioness she wore a great many jewels including a tiara and necklace of turquoises and diamonds.

There was no need for words for the Duke to know how pleased she was to see him, or that like him she was excited that they were together and there would be no restrictions to their enjoyment.

As the Duke took her hand in his he felt her fingers at first quiver, then tighten, and he thought Goodwood Races would mean a great deal to him this year, and not only on the race-course.

There was a party of twenty staying in the house.

The Duke as the most important guest present gave his hostess his arm and led her into the Dining-Room saying as he did so:

"It is delightful to find so many of my close friends staying under your roof."

"I thought that was what you would say," the Marchioness replied, "and what is so gratifying is that they are my friends too!"

The Duke knew that this was a compliment, and as if she was determined to emphasise the obvious, the Marchioness went on:

"I have known Fenella Newbury since she was a girl, but I have never seen her look more lovely than she does at the moment."

The Duke knew exactly what she was insinuating but he only replied:

"I have always thought the newspapers are right when they say that not only the best horses are to be seen at Goodwood, but also the most beautiful women."

The food at dinner was excellent, the wines superb and the Duke found himself enjoying the conversation which seemed to sparkle like champagne.

There were also the unspoken thoughts he exchanged with Fenella Newbury.

He was on his hostess's right with her on his other side, and he found the little asides they made to each other besides the exchange of glances grew more intimate as dinner progressed.

The Duke had noticed when they sat down that Aldora was at the other end of the table seated between two younger men, and he was extremely glad that she was nowhere near him.

Halfway through the meal he looked towards her without really meaning to and found she was looking at him.

He was aware again of the hatred in her eyes that had been so disturbing when they met in the Park, and seemed very out of place in such congenial company.

It was certainly unprecedented for a woman to look at him in such a manner.

In fact it made him forget what he was talking about at that particular moment and he found himself wondering how it was possible for his reputation to have come to the knowledge of a girl who could only just have left the School-Room, and why it should have upset her.

"The whole thing is ridiculous!" he thought. 'A child of that age should not know about anybody's love-affairs, and certainly should not be affected by them.'

In the Social World in which he moved nobody was shocked by an *affaire de coeur* and the only person likely to be annoyed by it was a discomfited husband.

It came as a surprise to the Duke that anybody so young and outside the orbit of his particular friends should be aware of his love-affairs and be censorious of them.

'I suppose she had listened to her mother's friends,' he thought scornfully, 'or else overheard the gossip of servants.'

Even so, as he was always particularly careful of the reputation of any lady with whom he was currently involved, it annoyed him to think that Aldora might be aware that he was interested in Fenella Newbury.

The Duke prided himself not only on his discretion, but on being very protective of a Lady's good name.

He had been known to walk out out of his Club if a woman was mentioned disparagingly by other members, and he never listened to gossip or encouraged it in his own house.

He found himself remembering now how Aldora had said that he treated women like oranges, sucked them dry and threw them away.

It was a vulgar way of speaking that he very much disliked, and he thought it was something nobody else would have had the temerity to say to him.

"You are looking worried," Fenella Newbury said very softly in his ear.

He thrust away the scowl between his eyes and turned to her with a smile.

"Forgive me," he said. "You know that all I want to do is to talk to you and listen to your very lovely voice."

"That is what I want you to do," she said very softly.

As her mouth moved sensuously over the words the Duke knew how much she wanted him to kiss her.

The dinner was a long-drawn-out meal, and when the ladies withdrew to the Drawing-Room Fenella Newbury said beneath her breath as she passed the Duke:

"Do not be too long."

"Of course not," he replied.

The Marchioness had already asked him, since there was no host at the party, if he would do the honours and bring the gentlemen into the Drawing-Room when they had finished their port.

The Duke did not like port and had only a small glass of brandy.

He was therefore soon ready to leave the table, to the surprise of some of his friends who had not yet finished their cigars.

One or two of them however looked knowingly at each other as he led the way to the Drawing-Room.

There the ladies of the party were elegantly draped on chairs and sofas like roses in full bloom.

There were green baize tables in the next room for those who preferred cards, and the Duke, hearing music as he entered the Drawing-Room, saw that Aldora was seated at the piano.

He thought with a sense of relief that that disposed of her. At the same time he was aware that she played surprisingly well for an *amateur*.

He looked around, saw Fenella Newbury sitting on a sofa alone, and knew from the way she eagerly lifted her eyes to his that she was waiting for him to join her.

As he sat down he was aware that the music had altered and as he heard the Mozart sonato Aldora had been playing being skilfully transformed into something light and romantic he had the uncomfortable feeling that she was mocking him.

"Damn the girl!" he said to himself. "If she were my daughter I would give her a good spanking and send her to bed!"

He however responded to the flattering things Fenella Newbury was saying to him and to the appreciation in her eyes.

But however determined he was not to listen, he was hearing the seductive melody of a Strauss Waltz telling him almost as if Aldora was saying it aloud that he was plucking yet another orange from the tree.

Try to ignore her as he would, The Duke found himself conscious of her all through the evening.

It was only when it was nearly midnight that he saw her rise from the piano to speak to her mother, and thought with a sigh of relief that she was leaving.

His assumption was correct for the Marchioness had obviously given Aldora permission to go to bed.

She went towards the door and only as she reached it did she look back to where the Duke was sitting, and almost as if she willed him, his eyes met hers.

They were quite some distance from each other, but as she stood there he saw incredibly that she turned her eyes inwards in the hideous, disfiguring squint that had appalled him when he had first seen her on the drive.

Then, while he could still hardly believe what he had seen, she had slipped through the door and was gone.

"It is growing late," Fenella Newbury was saying, "and as we shall have a long day at the races tomorrow, I think I should . . . retire."

She looked at him as she spoke, then so softly he could only just hear her she whispered:

"I am in the Stuart Room opposite yours!"

She rose to her feet and as she did so several other ladies, as if at a given signal, rose too and began saying goodnight to their hostess.

The gentlemen did not linger long after the ladies had left the Drawing-Room.

Some of them had come long distances, and like the Duke, although it was now possible to reach Goodwood by train, they all preferred to drive.

It was a race-meeting to which most of the aristocratic race-goers took their own coaches, using them to watch from rather than the stands and having luncheon in them.

Whether they had driven to Berkhampton House by coach, Phaeton or carriage, the dust along the twisting lanes in the vicinity of Goodwood made the last part of the journey very tiring.

His valet was waiting in his bedroom and having undressed the Duke put on a long robe which reached to the ground, and dismissed the man.

He walked across the room to draw back the curtains from one of the windows and looked out into the night.

The gardens sloping down to a lake were very beautiful and the stars filled the sky.

There was a half-moon rising above the trees in the Park, and seeing the drive reminded the Duke once again of Aldora and the violent manner in which she had denounced him.

"One thing is quite obvious," he told himself, "the Marchioness has no designs on me as a son-in-law, and the company, with the exception of her daughter, had been chosen to please my taste and make certain I enjoy myself."

Not only was he paired with Fenella, and he wondered vaguely how the Marchioness was already aware that he was interested in her, but his men-friends were all provided with the lady of their choice.

Several of these ladies were accompanied by their husbands, but in those cases, amusement for the husbands was also supplied.

Thinking it over the Duke realised that the Marchioness's guests must be thinking exactly as he was, that she knew just what each person wanted and like a Fairy-Godmother had waved her magic wand:

It suddenly flashed through his mind that it was all too contrived, and it was almost as if her guests were puppets and the Marchioness was pulling the strings.

He found himself as he looked at the stars wondering what it would be like if just one woman whom he wanted, was out of reach and he knew she was unobtainable.

He smiled and thought it had never happened so far in his life, and was unlikely to happen in the future.

Fenella was certainly not out of reach but waiting for him, doubtless impatiently.

Quite unexpectedly the idea came into his mind of going straight to bed instead of doing just what was expected of him.

In fact, everything seemed to have been planned so smoothly, that it was almost like gliding down-stream and having to make no effort to use an oar.

Then he thought he was being ridiculous.

Fenella was one of the most beautiful women he had ever seen, and she attracted him as he knew he attracted her.

"Why am I hesitating?" he asked himself angrily.

He drew the curtains and shut out the light.

The Duke always rose early.

Whatever time he got to bed the night before, he always awoke on the stroke of six o'clock, and even if he tried he found it impossible to go to sleep again.

Sometimes, if the weather was bad and he was in London, he would stay in bed and read a book. But these occasions were so rare that wherever he was his grooms always had a horse ready for him at exactly six-fifteen.

This morning, although the Duke as might be expected, had had very little sleep, he did not feel in the least tired.

Fenella had been all he had anticipated, eager and passionate, but in many ways unawakened to the full possibilities of love-making at which the Duke was such an expert.

He thought however as he washed in cold water that he disliked an exotic perfume which lingered on his skin.

As he scrubbed himself rather harder than usual he looked forward to riding over the beautiful countryside that enthralled him every time he came here.

Therefore he entered the stables just before a quarter past six o'clock and as he appeared his own grooms led a grey stallion that he had sent ahead of him into the yard.

It was a horse he had not owned for long and which was still fighting against acknowledging his master.

The Duke's eyes brightened. He knew that he was going to enjoy the age-old battle between man and beast and that his stallion would undoubtedly present a challenge.

He leapt into the saddle and was just about to ride out of the yard when he was aware that in a field nearby somebody else was riding, and at that moment jumping a very high fence.

It was so high that the Duke thought for a moment that the horse must have wings to attempt it, and as it sailed over the top thought it must fall on landing.

Instead it reached the ground without mishap and as horse and rider moved on he realised that there was a woman in the saddle.

"Who is that?" he asked sharply.

The groom in charge of the stables replied:

"That be Lady Aldora, Your Grace. 'Er Ladyship's 'ad fences erected the same 'eight as they at t'National Steeple Chase, an' 'ers training three 'orses over them."

The Duke could hardly believe what he had heard.

The fences at the National Steeple Chase at Liverpool were the highest of any race-course in the country, and it was inconceivable that they should be jumped by a woman rider.

Without saying any more he turned his horse and rode out from the stable-yard into the paddock beyond it where he could now see the jumps erected in a huge circle the width of two fields.

Aldora, having taken two other fences while he was

talking, was now as far away from him as the course allowed, and was taking what he was aware was a replica of the water-jump.

She rode her horse at the fence and as he leapt the Duke was almost certain that he would land in the water on the other side of it.

But as if Aldora compelled him to do so, he stretched out at the last moment and avoided calamity by a hair's breadth.

There were two more fences before Aldora would be back to where he was watching her.

As he had no wish to accompany his hostess's daughter, who he was still convinced was slightly touched in the head, the best thing he could do, he told himself, was to ride off in the opposite direction.

But because the two fences that were still to be jumped were very high, he was somehow compelled to watch Aldora taking them in a manner which he had to admit he could not have bettered himself.

After the last jump as she came trotting towards him, he saw her pat her horse's neck and talk to him with a smile on her lips which brought her dimples into play.

"You are a clever boy and I am very pleased with you!" the Duke heard her say.

Then as she suddenly saw him, he realised she stiffened, the smile and her dimples disappeared, and the hostile expression was back in her eyes.

He did not move and only when after a few steps her horse was close to his did he somewhat perfunctorily lift his hat.

"You are up very early!" she remarked. "I should have thought you would be too fatigued to ride!"

As if she had told him blatantly that she knew how he had spent the night, and with whom, the Duke for a moment was too astonished to be angry.

Then she would have passed him without saying any more, if he had not said:

"I suppose I can only congratulate you on taking fences which most men would be afraid to tackle."

"I expect Johnson told you they are a replica of the National Steeple Chase?"

"He did, but surely you are risking, if not your life, your limbs in training inexperienced horses over them?"

"They have to learn sometime," Aldora replied, "and actually the fences are made lower until they gain experience and confidence."

The Duke was aware that she was conversing with him reluctantly, but because they were talking of horses, felt she must reply truthfully to his question.

After a moment he said:

"I would like to try my own horse over them, but quite frankly, as he is not fully trained and has never jumped anything to my knowledge that is half the height, I am rather reluctant to risk it."

He was really talking to himself, and as he finished speaking he expected Aldora to jeer at him for being a coward.

That was what he might anticipate from her, he thought, but to his surprise she said:

"Of course you must not risk your neck or your stallion's until he has had more experience, but if you would like to try *Red Rufus* he takes them perfectly, and I intend to enter him next year at Liverpool."

She did not wait for the Duke to agree but gave the order to one of the stable-boys.

A few minutes later he brought to the Duke's side a large chestnut which he saw at a glance was not a particularly showy animal, but had the length of leg that made him a good jumper.

He had not spoken to Aldora while they were waiting, but merely sat looking at the fences, appraising them and calculating exactly the manner in which he should take his mount over each one of them.

When he was in the saddle on *Red Rufus* he realised that Aldora had been right in saying that the horse was experienced and completely at home.

He sailed over the jumps with an inch or two to spare in each case, and leapt the water with ease.

The whole performance gave the Duke a feeling of exhilaration and he had to admit delight.

Never could he remember taking such high jumps or so many of them in quick succession.

As he trotted back towards Aldora who was waiting for him, he knew that however abominable she might be he had to be grateful to her for an unusual experience.

"Thank you," he said, "and again I must congratulate you. I feel sure *Red Rufus* will come up to all your expectations."

"Only if I am fortunate enough to be there," she replied.

The Duke remounted his own stallion and knew she was referring once again to her absurd idea that her mother intended him to be her husband.

Because the knowledge annoyed him, he merely lifted his hat and rode away in the direction he had intended to go in the first place.

"She may be mad in some respects," he told himself, "but she can certainly ride better than any woman I have ever seen!"

There were no ladies at breakfast when the Duke returned to the house and the conversation was entirely on what horses should be backed during the day.

The Duke was already confident that he would win the Stewards' Cup, but as he had no wish to shorten the odds against his horse any further, he said very little.

Only when the ladies, looking extremely beautiful in their elegant gowns and carrying small sunshades to protect their complexions, came down the stairs to where the coaches which would carry them to the Race Course were waiting, did he know that it would be his duty to see that Fenella backed all the winners.

She was looking exceedingly lovely, wearing again her favourite blue, but her hat was trimmed with pink roses, and her sunshade was also decorated with them.

The expression in her eyes told the Duke that she was very much in love with him, and already their love-affair had passed the preliminary stage of an exciting flirtation and had embarked on what could, as he knew only too well from the past, become of he was not careful a stormy sea of deep and tempestuous emotion.

Last night had been such a familiar pleasure that he had not thought about it while he was riding.

Now he remembered with a sudden irritation that, even in the most passionate moments of his love-making with Fenella, at the back of his mind he had been uncomfortably aware of Aldora's condemnation.

He tried to force himself not to think about it, and yet in some manner that he could not control, as Fenella looked at him with what he knew all too well was an unmistakable expression of love, he found himself thinking of Aldora.

He saw now to his discomfort that she was one of the party in the same coach as himself.

It was some consolation that she sat as far away from him as it was possible to be, and made no attempt to speak to him.

At the same time he found it difficult not to be aware that she was present, and knew that if he met her eyes they would be hating him in the same way as they had last night.

It was only when this morning she was speaking of horses that she had spoken to him naturally, but coldly and impersonally as if he was a complete stranger.

"She is spoiling the whole party for me!" he told himself.

He did not ask himself how one young and unimportant girl should be capable of such a remarkable feat.

* * *

There were three miles of twisting, dusty lanes before they reached the gates of Goodwood Park and finally drew up in front of the house where there was a large marquee.

The horses were stamping their feet and twitching their tails to avoid the flies under the trees, and the Duke saw a green Landau with four bays, the postilions in red and white striped jackets.

There were coachmen in similar liveries waiting to convey the Duke of Richmond's party to the stands.

However the Berkhampton party arrived first and were welcomed by footmen in white and red liveries turned up with silver and turned down with yellow.

They brought drinks for those who needed them and arranged cushions behind the seats of each of the ladies who sat elegantly looking like bouquets of flowers.

Everything at Goodwood was planned to make it seem just a private party taking place in the private Park, and the Duke found himself agreeing with some of the more effusive newspapers that carried a sporting page.

But he was so interested in the racing and the horses taking part that he invariably found that women, however beautiful, were somewhat of an encumbrance at a race-meeting.

He was well aware that Fenella, although she was very anxious to please him, knew little or nothing about horses, and was only interested so long as it concerned himself.

This was a characteristic of almost every woman with whom he had had an *affaire de coeur*, so it did not surprise him.

At the same time he noticed that Aldora, although he was certain it was highly unconventional, was talking to the jockeys before and after the races, and spent her time inspecting the horses in the paddock rather than gossiping in the stands.

As he happened to bump into her in a doorway just before one of the races, he asked, almost as if he could not help himself:

"Have you had any luck?"

"First and second in every race so far!" she replied. "But then I am a red flag to the Bookies, as you are a red flag to me!"

He saw her dimples before with her parting shot she hurried away from him.

He thought once again that she should be given a good spanking, kept in the School-Room, and not allowed to associate with grown-ups.

Because he felt a little piqued he sat down beside Fenella as they waited for the horses to go to the starting-point.

He tried to tell her a little about his own horse which he was quite certain would win the race, and which he had trained himself.

But before he could begin she started to tell him how much he meant to her, and to make it very clear that the only conversation which really interested her was one that concerned them both and their feelings towards each other.

The Duke was compelled almost rudely to rise to his feet in the middle of what might have been called a 'declaration of love' as the horses were off.

The going was rough, but the horses taking part in the race were all exceptionally well-trained and although the Duke was almost certain he would be the winner, it was a very close finish.

In fact, as they passed the post he thought it was a dead-heat only to learn with a sense of elation that his horse had won by a nose.

It was one of the most exciting races he had watched for some time.

However there was a distinctly bored note in Fenella's voice as she asked when it was over:

"Did you win?"

"We are waiting for the Judges' decision," Duke said sharply.

He watched her take a tiny mirror from her reticule and

he was aware that, like so many other women, she was not interested in the racing only in the man to whom the horses belonged.

When he reached the gate onto the course, it was to find that amongst the crowd clustered there was Aldora.

She was chatting in what he thought was a far too familiar manner to some disreputable-looking racing characters who gave a cheer as he appeared, saying:

"Thank ye, thank ye! Us might have knowd Yer Grace'd not fail us!"

"I suppose they backed the winner," the Duke remarked to Aldora.

"Of course they did!" she replied. "I had a look at *Hercules* before the race started, and I told them he would win, even though it was a close shave!"

"We're ever so grateful to Yer Ladyship," one of the men said, "But then ye never fails us. What do ye fancy for the next race?"

It annoyed the Duke in a way that surprised him that Aldora should talk of the horses in the next race as if she was familiar with every one of them.

Then she said:

"I cannot tell you for certain until the last moment, but on form it should be *'Gordon'*."

"We're not interested in form," one of the men said, "wot us wants to know is what ye thinks clairvoyant-like. That's wot brings 'ome the bacon!"

As the man said the world 'clairvoyant' the Duke looked at Aldora sharply.

He could hardly believe that she was talking gypsy nonsense to these men.

He thought once again it was extremely reprehensible that she should be wandering about the course instead of sitting in the box beside her mother as she should be doing.

Then as he was about to tell her so, he decided it was not his business and the less he had to do with such a tiresome girl the better.

However he noticed that she did not come back to the box to watch the race until all the horses had gone up to the start.

He also thought he could see her still talking to her disreputable friends long after he had taken his place by Fenella.

Aldora was sitting at the back of the box and he wondered whether it was because she was not particularly interested in seeing what happened in this race.

Then just as the starter gave the 'off' and the horses surged forward he was aware that Aldora had climbed onto a chair so that she could see over the heads of those in front.

Again he thought it reprehensible behaviour for a young lady, but the Marchioness did not appear to notice what her daughter was doing.

Only when the horses came down the straight and a complete outsider came galloping home a length ahead of the rest of the field did the Duke hear a cheer behind him and know it came from Aldora.

He could hardly believe that she had been able to tip the winner of this race!

When later he went round to the paddock, he found himself against his better judgement going up to her as she was watching the horses parading for the fourth race and asking:

"Were you lucky last time? I can hardly believe you were!"

She did not look at him but continued to watch intently the horses parading past her as she replied:

"Yes, I knew at the last minute that *'Golden Sunset'* would win!"

"How did you know?"

There was silence. Then after a moment the Duke said:

"I asked you a question! How did you know?"

She looked up at him and her voice was quite sincere as she replied:

"I cannot explain it, but it is something I do know and I am seldom wrong!"

"Are you really saying that you can prognosticate clairvoyantly, as your friends said, what is going to be the winner of a race?"

"Only when I have seen the horses and been close to them!"

Aldora spoke as if she was hardly attending to the question and the Duke said sharply:

"Explain it to me, I do not understand!"

"There is nothing to understand," Aldora replied. "Either one has what the gypsies call *'The Eye'*, or one has not."

"And it is something you have?"

"Yes."

"I suppose it is something I do not possess!"

She turned her face to look at him as if for the first time, and he saw that her eyes, although they were grey, had little flecks of gold in them as if the sunshine had become imprisoned there.

She looked at him for a long moment and he had the strange feeling that she was looking into him rather than at him.

Then she said:

"Because you know a lot about horses and they mean so much to you, it might be possible for you to develop it. But as you do not believe, I think it is very unlikely."

"Believe what?" the Duke asked.

Unexpectedly Aldora smiled, and he saw her dimples.

"That, Your Grace," she said mockingly, "you must find out for yourself!"

She walked away as if she had dismissed him from her mind.

The Duke found himself thinking that never in his

experience had any woman ended a conversation so abruptly, or left him when he wanted to go on talking to her.

He did not see Aldora again until after the last race she came hurrying up to the coach when everybody else was already in it and ready to leave.

As she reached it she turned round to wave to what appeared to be a large number of her friends.

The Duke heard them cheer her and some of the men waved their hats.

As she sat down in the coach it moved off, and the Duke found himself wondering what the Marchioness thought of her daughter's behaviour.

Surprisingly she did not seem perturbed or even interested.

That night there were thirty guests to join the house-party after dinner.

The Duke was not surprised to find there was a large Ball-Room attached to the house at the back and an excellent Orchestra had come from London.

Fenella was entranced at the thought of being able to dance with him.

"It is something I have longed to do ever since I first saw you," she said.

"I can hold you in my arms without having to be on a Ball-Room floor," he replied.

"I want both," she answered, "and I know you dance as you do everything else – divinely!"

There was a little pause before the last three words and an unmistakable innuendo in her voice.

The Duke accepted such compliments as his right, and it struck him that while he had so many talents it was rather annoying that he did not have 'The Eye', as Aldora called it.

He was sure it was all nonsense and he did not believe in magic powers or supernatural happenings of any sort.

And yet it was extraordinary that Aldora should have

tipped *Golden Sunset* which had started, he discovered later, at 40-1 against.

"There must be some crookery about it," he told himself suspiciously.

And yet, if there were, how could a well-brought-up young débutante, who should be sheltered and cosseted, know anything about it?

As a member of the Jockey Club he was well aware of the irregular practices that took place on most race-courses, and which were difficult to discern and impossible to prevent.

But he could not believe any Lady could have any knowledge of them.

If however it was some perceptive instinct which told Aldora what the winners would be, it could doubtless prove a very lucrative gift as obviously some of her dubious admirers on the race-course had discovered.

"40-1!" he murmured to himself.

Then he remembered that nearly every member of the house-party had backed the favourite and lost money.

When he saw Aldora at dinner he knew that once again she was beautifully dressed, and her mother certainly made the best of her looks.

Tonight she was wearing a very pale green gown, the colour of the buds of spring, and there was a wreath of leaves on her fair hair.

It somehow gave her an elfin look which made the Duke think she seemed part of the trees under which he had first met her, and that she was more at home out of doors than she was in a Ball-Room.

He did not know why this thought came to him, except that he could still see her in his mind's eye taking the immensely high fences she had jumped that morning.

In some way he could not explain she lifted her horse over them as if she gave it wings.

"I do not want to think about the girl," the Duke told himself.

Then he was aware that as she waltzed around the room with a handsome young Officer in the Brigade of Guards, she was laughing spontaneously and it was a genuine sound that again belonged to the woods or the garden.

When they had finished dancing Fenella drew him through one of the open windows onto the lawn outside.

Just as he had seen last night before he went to her room, the stars filled the sky, but the moon was bigger than it had been then.

As they walked away from the house and Fenella drew nearer to him he knew she was wanting his kisses and as soon as they reached the shadows she would throw herself into his arms.

It passed through his mind that like so many women she was moving too quickly. She should be waiting for his advances and make it more exciting by pretending to be a little reluctant, rather than over-eager.

It was then as they reached the other side of a yew-hedge that Fenella stopped still and with the moonlight on her face, looked up at him.

"Oh, darling!" she said in a voice that seemed as caressing as if she touched him, "it has been a long, long day before we could be together!"

The Duke looked at her and thought she was undoubtedly one of the most beautiful women he had ever seen.

Yet at the moment he could view her dispassionately and actually he had no particular desire to touch her.

Then as she was aware of his hesitation she flung her arms round his neck, pulling his head down to hers.

He could feel the softness of her body against his and the exotic scent she used was in his nostrils.

Still there was no response within him until her lips were on his, passionate, insistent, pleading, and demanding all at the same time.

She held him closer and at last he was aware that she had excited him and he wanted her as a man wants a woman.

Then as he kissed her as she wanted him to do and he felt her pulsating in his arms, it flashed through the Duke's mind that perhaps Aldora was aware of what was happening, and was condemning him for it with hatred in her eyes.

CHAPTER THREE

The second day's racing followed much the same course as the first, with the coaches taking the party to the course and the horses being if anything, more spectacular than on the previous day.

That also applied to the ladies' clothes, for their bustles seemed to grow in size, their bonnets and hats to be more profusedly trimmed, and their faces seemed even lovelier.

The Duke naturally was interested in the horses, and because this kept him away from the box for so long Fenella was pouting when he returned.

When he sat down beside her she touched him with her hands and looked at him in a manner which he thought was indiscreet.

If the Duke was careful of the reputation of the ladies with whom he amused himself, he was just as careful of his own.

He could not help people talking about him, but he had no desire to furnish fresh grounds for gossip or to feed their imaginations which he was well aware were very fertile.

He therefore went to talk to a number of men who were standing at the back of the box.

While he was there he was aware that at the very last moment, just before the race started, Aldora had slipped in at the back and positioned herself beside the chair on which she intended to stand to watch it.

Almost as though he could not help himself he said to her:

"I hope your 'Eye' had told you that *Foxhunter* will win the Queen's Plate."

Foxhunter was his own horse, and having been heavily backed was now 'odds on'.

To his annoyance he found himself waiting almost apprehensively for her reply. Finally, as if the words came from her lips reluctantly, Aldora said:

"I have backed *'Terrier'*!"

The Duke stared at her in astonishment.

He had gone through the race-card very carefully and the only horse that was a complete and absolute outsider and belonged to an owner whose name he did not recognise was *Terrier*.

All the others were known to him for their breeding, for their owners, and for their form on a great many other race-courses.

It was then he decided he was taking her pretensions at 'tipping the winner' far too seriously, and he felt she was just playing about in what should be a man's pastime, not a woman's.

She was well aware that his lips curled cynically before he said in a voice that was very eloquent of his thoughts:

"I can only wish you luck!"

He walked back to his seat beside Fenella and realised as he did so that the horses were 'off' and that everybody was leaning forward excitedly.

His only real interest in the race was whether his horse would beat the Duke of Richmond's, who was extremely proud of an animal that had already brought him during the year, a considerable sum in prize-money.

It was not the money that counted on this occasion.

It was, as far as the Duke of Richmond was concerned, the joy of winning with his own horse on his own race-course and beating his own friends.

The Duke could appreciate such feelings in an owner. At the same time, he was very anxious to prove that *Foxhunter* was as excellent as he thought him to be.

He knew that everybody in his stable was backing him, as

were all the guests at Berkhampton House.

"You must not disappoint us tomorrow, Ingram!" they had said to him last night. "We are relying on you to make us our expenses for the whole meeting!"

The Duke knew that this meant they expected him to win the Queen's Plate as well as the Goodwood Cup.

He did not think of Aldora's choice again until the horses reached the straight the second time round.

He was then aware that riding close beside his colours and those of the Duke of Richmond there was a jockey wearing an unfamiliar combination of green and yellow spots with a green cap and cross-belts.

He put his glasses to his eyes and told himself this must be *Terrier*.

The horse was on the small side but going well, and he had a kind of wiry look about him which accounted for his name.

Then as the Duke realised his own jockey was straining every nerve to get ahead of the Duke of Richmond's horse, *Terrier* unobtrusively slipped past them both.

To the astonishment of the crowd who watched almost in silence he swept past the winning-post a length ahead of the two favourites.

There was an audible gasp from the box and as everybody began to commiserate with the Duke in a very half-hearted manner because they had themselves lost money, he looked around to see whether Aldora was gloating over him.

The chair however on which she had been standing was empty, and he guessed that she had gone down to see the horse she had tipped led in.

He knew there was no hurry for him and moved towards the Marchioness who said in her soft, sympathetic voice:

"I am so sorry, Ingram, but I am sure you will make up for it tomorrow by winning the Goodwood Cup!"

"I am only sorry for those who followed me," the Duke replied somewhat stiffly.

He then joined the other gentlemen who were proceeding down to the course.

There was no sign of Aldora and as he walked towards the Weighing-In Room he saw the boards go up to show that his own horse and the Duke of Richmond's had dead-heated for second place.

It was a poor consolation, and he was not surprised a moment later to see Aldora talking animatedly to a middle-aged man who had just led in the winner of the race.

Because the Duke was always courteous he went up to him and said:

"I believe you must be Mr. Barnard, and may I congratulate you on a magnificent win which was certainly a great surprise!"

"I thank Your Grace! I was as surprised as everybody else!" Mr. Barnard replied, "except of course, Lady Aldora."

The Duke looked at Aldora and thought her smile and her dimples were mocking at him.

Then as Mr. Barnard was surrounded by people congratulating him, he asked as if he could not prevent himself from doing so:

"How could you have known that *Terrier*, which is not a very spectacular horse, would win?"

She did not answer and he said with what was undoubtedly a sneer in his voice:

"You may tell me it is your 'Eye', but I shall still think you must have other ways of ascertaining matters of which the ordinary race-goers are ignorant."

She did not reply, and as his horse came riding in from the course with the Duke of Richmond's, both jockeys looking somewhat crestfallen, she said almost as if the Duke was condemning them:

"They did their best!"

"I am aware of that," he said sharply.

Almost as if she spurred him to do so, he said to his jockey:

"Bad luck, Davis, but one can never account for the unknown and the unexpected."

The jockey grinned ruefully.

"I'm sorry, Yer Grace. I did me best, but I know ye be disappointed."

"There is always tomorrow," the Duke replied.

He patted his horse and turned away to find himself thinking that perhaps tomorrow would be another disappointment. Aldora might have something up her sleeve which against all expectations would win the Goodwood Cup.

Although he tried to put her out of his mind, the Duke found himself thinking of her during the evening.

He found it incredible that in two days of racing she had tipped complete and absolute outsiders with an expertise which any member of the Jockey Club would envy.

He decided to talk to her again, and try to find out more about how she did it. Was it really some gypsy magic or, if she preferred, clairvoyant perception that he had never met before?

He told himself she was in any case, an abominable young woman and, although he did not believe a word of what she had warned him was her mother's intention, it would certainly be a mistake for him to show any interest in her.

All the same what he could not help noticing was that she looked very attractive in a different way from any other of the lovely women present.

What was more, the other members of the house-party who danced with her, seemed to be fascinated by what she had to say.

Later in the evening, when he walked into the Drawing-Room in search of a glass of champagne, he saw Aldora sitting beside an elderly Ambassador who had been asked, he thought, because he was one of the Marchioness's special friends.

They were talking very earnestly and as he passed them he heard the Ambassador say:

"The Russian intention is quite clear to the India Office, and the Prime Minister is extremely worried, especially as Lord Northbrook has made such a mess over our relationship with Sher Ali."

The Duke thought it was a most extraordinary conversation for the Ambassador to be having with a young girl and he deliberately slowed his pace to hear what Aldora would reply.

"I hear," she said in her soft, clear voice, "that Lord Northbrook is retiring for domestic reasons."

"If that is true," the Ambassador answered, "it is the best thing that could possibly happen."

"It is true," Aldora said, "as you will learn in a day or so."

The Duke thought it would be a mistake to eaves'-drop any further, but he could hardly believe what he had heard.

How could Aldora, who must be only just eighteen, be talking in such a manner to the Ambassador, who he had known for some years, and for whom he had a great respect?

He felt as he filled his glass that if the conversation had been repeated to him he would not have believed it, and would have thought somebody was pulling his leg.

Then as he returned with the drink in his hand to the card-room, he was aware that Aldora had risen from the sofa on which she had been sitting beside the Ambassador and was crossing the Drawing-Room obviously on her way to bed.

Because he could not help being curious the Duke stopped beside the Ambassador to say:

"Can I bring you a drink, Your Excellency?"

"No, thank you," the Ambassador replied. "I am going to find my hostess and hope she will forgive me for being tired after a long day's racing."

"I heard you talking very seriously to our hostess's youngest daughter," the Duke remarked.

"A brilliant girl," the Ambassador murmured, "absolutely brilliant! It is a terrible pity she was not a boy!"

57

He walked away as he spoke, leaving the Duke staring after him in astonishment.

Then he told himself that his impression of Aldora was a very different one, and the Ambassador must have been fooled, as older men often were, by a pretty face.

The next morning the Duke went riding at his usual time.

He half-expected to find Aldora either schooling her horses over the jumps or somewhere in the stables.

But to his surprise and with what he recognised as a slight irritation there was no sign of her.

He would not demean himself to ask where she was, but instead rode off into the Park, over the flat fields and on towards the rolling downs.

Although he rode for over two hours there was no sign of Aldora.

Only when he came back into the stable-yard did he see her horse, who looked as if he had taken some extremely strenuous exercise, being led into the stables.

The Duke decided that Aldora must be deliberately avoiding him.

Then he told himself that was what he wanted.

He was aware at the same time that he would have liked to question her more closely about the races.

It was very hot, even for the end of July, and because of the temperature everybody seemed a little more on edge than they had been the previous day.

As the horses paraded round the paddock the Duke thought he had never seen *Meteor* whom he had entered for the Queen's Plate, look better.

He felt confident that he would win, and knew his jockey felt the same.

Then as the horses began to go down to the start he came upon Aldora walking away from a group of her strange friends.

She did not see him because she was looking down at her

race-card, a little frown between her eyes.

The Duke stopped deliberately in her path.

"Am I to expect bad news, or good?" he asked in a tone of somebody patronising a young child.

She looked up at him and there was just a faint smile on her lips as she replied:

"I am sure Your Grace, that it would spoil your enjoyment during the race if you knew what would be the conclusion."

"What you are really saying," the Duke replied almost aggressively, "is that you do not know, and therefore will not speculate."

She looked at him in a manner that told him she was amused by what he was saying, and understood that what had happened the previous day had made him slightly apprehensive.

Then without saying anything she walked away, leaving him staring after her.

'I find the girl abominably rude, unpredictable and extremely tiresome,' he thought.

Once again, although he tried not to think about it, he knew that when he had been with Fenella last night he had the uncomfortable feeling that Aldora was aware of it and was shocked by his behaviour.

'I made a mistake in coming to Berkhampton House,' he thought as he walked back to the stand. 'Another year I shall go to the Richmonds, as I always have!'

He reached the box, sat down beside Fenella, and as her gloved hand went out to touch his arm, she said:

"I am sure, dearest, that *Meteor* will win, and I do hope you have backed it for me!"

"Yes, of course," the Duke replied.

He had actually forgotten to do anything of the sort and as he seldom bet on his own horses had not gone near the Bookies.

"Thank you," Fenella said, "and I hope you will buy a

special present for me so that we shall never forget how very, very happy we have been at Berkhampton House."

It was the sort of thing, because the Duke was so rich, that women always said to him and it never failed to irritate him.

In fact, he was extremely generous and never forgot to reward them for their favours, with a very handsome piece of jewellery, just as he rewarded his current mistress in cash.

He always felt that women showed lack of tact and finesse if their greed was too obvious, and he thought that, beautiful though she was, if he spent too much time with Fenella she would begin to pall on him.

Then he had the uncomfortable feeling that Aldora at the back of the box would be aware of what he was thinking and know that yet another orange was nearly sucked dry!

When they returned to Berkhampton House there as a telegram for Fenella and instantly there was consternation and where she was concerned, almost a scene.

Lord Newbury had telegraphed his wife that his mother had suffered a heart-attack and was at death's door.

He ordered Fenella to return to London immediately, and as the quickest way to travel was by train the Marchioness said she would have her driven to Chichester where she could catch an express.

"I will see you off," the Duke said, feeling there was nothing else he could do.

He saw the tears in Fenella's eyes as she had thanked him.

Amazingly, she was ready in an hour, although some of her heavier luggage would have to follow her later.

They set off in one of the Marchioness's comfortable carriages, and the whole four miles to Chichester was spent by Fenella in reiterating over and over again to the Duke how much she loved him.

She was obviously devestated at having to leave him when they might have had two more nights together, and there was little he could say to comfort her.

He kissed her good-bye in the carriage, and on the

platform he raised her hand to his lips.

Comfortably ensconced in a reserved carriage Fenella was borne away from him with the traditional waving of the red flag, clouds of steam, and the noise of porters slamming the carriage doors as the train began to move.

He had a last glimpse of her lovely face as she leaned out of the window to smile at him.

Replacing his hat on his head he walked briskly back to where the carriage was waiting.

Putting his feet up on the seat opposite him, he knew if he was truthful, that he had no regrets that Fenella had gone and he would enjoy the racing more without her.

He did not think it extraordinary that she should feel this way. The fact was, making love to Fenella was almost like eating too much *pâté de foie gras* and enough was enough.

His journey to Chichester and back meant that he had to hurry to dress for dinner, and when he came downstairs it was to find all the rest of the party had already assembled in the Drawing-Room.

He therefore had no chance to talk to his hostess alone or to wonder if Fenella's unexpected departure had upset the seating arrangement at the dinner-table.

He saw, however, there were a number of people dining who had not been there the night before.

While he waited to be told who he was taking in to dinner he heard the Marchioness's voice beside him saying:

"I am sorry, Ingram, that Fenella has had to leave us, and for this evening, I suggest that Aldora should take her place. I know that you will have a great bond in common with your love of horses, so you will have plenty to talk about."

The Duke unconsciously raised his eye-brows in surprise.

He had been eyeing the very attractive wife of the Lord Lieutenant who had married for the second time and her dark hair and flashing eyes had caught his attention.

But as the Marchioness moved ahead of him with the Ambassador Aldora was at his side and there was nothing he could do but offer her his arm.

"Too bad!" she said beneath her breath.

He had the uncomfortable feeling that she was well aware of what he was thinking.

The Duke however had no intention of lowering himself by being rude whatever Aldora might say.

As soon as he had exchanged a few pleasantries with his hostess for the conventional amount of time he turned to Aldora, hoping if she was going to be offensive that nobody else at the table would be aware of it.

Instead he found her deep in conversation with the man on her other side who was the local Master of Foxhounds.

He was aware they were discussing horses and in fact, having a spirited argument about them.

The Master of Foxhounds saw that the Duke's face was turned in his direction and said:

"Come and support me! I am on losing ground with Lady Aldora who, although I hate to admit it, knows more about horses than I do. She also has revolutionary ideas about the way we draw our covers."

Now the Duke was really aroused and found himself deeply involved in the argument.

He deliberately took the opposite view to Aldora, but he realised, although it was infuriating to be forced to admit it to himself, that she was right.

After dinner when the gentlemen joined the ladies the Marchioness said:

"Do not sit down at a card-table, Ingram, because I want to talk to you."

The Duke realised there were even numbers without him, and with Aldora playing the piano everybody was accounted for.

The Marchioness then slipped her arm through his and drew him from the Drawing-Room into a very comfortable Sitting-Room adjacent to it, which was particularly her own.

There were flowers everywhere including a profusion of rosebuds which filled the hearth.

The long windows were open into the garden and as the Duke felt rather tired he was glad he did not have to play Bridge and make conversation.

The Marchioness indicated with her hand a large and comfortable sofa, and as he sank down into it she brought him a glass of brandy and he took it from her with a smile.

"A very successful party!" he remarked.

"Thank you, but it was a pity that Fenella had to leave early," she said. "However that gives me an opportunity to talk to you now, and as tomorrow we are to dine with the Lord Lieutenant it may be more difficult."

The Duke sipped his brandy.

Then as if she had dropped a bomb-shell at his feet the Marchioness said quietly:

"I want to talk to you about Aldora!"

The Duke stiffened.

In spite of Aldora's warning he had thought, since Fenella was in the party and until this evening the Marchioness had never made any effort to bring them together, that what the girl had told him was merely nonsense.

He was convinced she was crazy on this point, if on nothing else.

"I do not suppose you are aware," the Marchioness was saying, "that Aldora is the Goddaughter of the Queen?"

The Duke murmured something appropriate and his hostess continued:

"It has also worried me that when she is twenty-one she comes into a very considerable fortune of her own which was left to her by another Godparent who died five years ago."

She glanced at the Duke to make sure he was listening.

"Aldora is very different from my other two daughters, and although it may seem incredible in so young a girl, she is brilliantly clever, so that we have never quite known what to do about her."

The Duke stared at the Marchioness as if he could not believe what he was hearing.

"Brilliantly clever?" he repeated.

"She already speaks six languages," the Marchioness replied, "and is now intent upon learning Russian. Apart from which she has a grasp of Politics and world affairs which, as I have told her often enough, is almost a pretention in so young a girl."

She gave a little laugh before she went on:

"It leads to awkward moments with Emissaries from other countries, and for that matter our own, for the simple reason that she always appears to know more than they do!"

It flashed through the Duke's mind that perhaps the Marchioness where her youngest daughter was concerned, was as deranged as he suspected Aldora of being.

Then he remembered that he had never heard anyone talk of the Marchioness without emphasising how intelligent she was, which accounted for her very powerful influence at Court.

He knew she was waiting for him to make some sort of comment and he murmured:

"You have certainly surprised me!"

As he spoke he was painfully aware of what was coming and wondered how he could possibly circumvent it.

Before he could find words to do so, the Marchioness went on:

"When I talked to the dear Queen about Aldora, she told me that she had alreay thought of a solution to my problem, and it concerns you!"

"Concerns me?" the Duke managed to say with a well-simulated note of surprise in his voice.

"Although it is strictly confidential to the members of the India Office at the moment," the Marchioness said, "the Viceroy Lord Northbrook is resigning and Her Majesty feels that in the very difficult relationship that exists between India and Afghanistan there could be nobody better qualified to deal with what might easily become a confrontation than yourself."

The Duke was so astonished that he could only stare at the Marchioness as if he could not believe what she had just said.

Then as she waited he asked:

"Are you seriously suggesting that Her Majesty intends to offer me the position of Viceroy of India?"

"That is what she is thinking of doing," the Marchioness replied, "but of course, as you are well aware, it is almost obligatory for the Viceroy to be married. Her Majesty therefore thinks that considering how clever Aldora is, she would in the circumstances prove exactly the right person to fulfil the duties of such a position."

For the first time in his life the Duke was literally bereft of speech.

He had never in his wildest dreams imagined himself as Viceroy of India.

He was well aware that it was the most important position that any man could achieve, since the Viceroy was in practice equal, if not superior, to any European King, and with a great deal more power than most of them.

He would be ruling over many hundred million people, and although he must consult the India Committee in London, he would have the final word in everything that occurred in that great country.

It flashed through his mind that no man could have a greater compliment paid to him than to be offered such a position.

With his genius for organisation he felt he would be able to do the task well, and what was more he would enjoy facing the many difficulties that would present themselves and perhaps would achieve a success such as no other Viceroy and certainly not Lord Northbrook, had been able to do.

Then almost as if a cascade of water had been poured over

him to sweep away the elation he was feeling, he knew that he would also be forced to accept Aldora as his wife.

It was not only that the Viceroy was expected to be married, although most of them were able to choose their own wives, it was that the Queen and the Marchioness together had made quite certain that the pill was there, even if it was deftly covered with jam.

He would either be the Viceroy with Aldora as his wife, or he would remain at home a bachelor and somebody else would be appointed to go to India and take Lord Northbrook's place.

The Duke was intelligent enough to realise there was no use arguing, and he had the feeling that it would be impossible to prevaricate.

It was a question of either accepting or refusing.

He put down the glass he was holding in his hand and rose to his feet to walk to the open window.

Outside there was the same magic of the moon and the stars, the silver of the lake and the fragrance of the flowers coming from the garden.

India was far away, England was here, and he already had a position in the Country that was second to none but the members of the Royal Family.

And yet he had been offered the most intriguing, the most exciting, and he was well aware the most difficult task in which to be successful, in the whole world.

There was no other position to equal it. It was equivalent, he thought, to winning every classic race that had ever been run, if he was to succeed against such formidable odds.

"Viceroy of India!"

He felt as if the Marchioness held out the prospect before his eyes, glittering like an enormous diamond that dazzled and mesmerised anybody who looked at it.

Then he saw Aldora, her eyes squinting, her mouth contorted, warning him that this would happen, and that he must refuse to marry her because she hated and despised him.

In what he felt was a weak voice because it was difficult to make it firm and positive the Duke asked:

"Have you spoken to your daughter about this, and asked her if she would be prepared to marry me?"

He turned as he spoke and saw the Marchioness's eyes flicker, which told him she had some idea of her daughter's feelings.

There was a perceptible pause before she replied:

"Aldora is very young and despite her brains is, in many ways, innocent of the world. But she will of course marry who I tell her to!"

The Duke thought the last sentence was spoken a little too quickly to be convincing.

"I think before I give you an answer to take to Her Majesty," he said a little pompously, "perhaps I should talk to Lady Aldora, and ask her if she is agreeable. Any Viceroy would find his work doubly hard if his wife were not in accordance with what he was doing."

The Marchioness looked down at the rings on her fingers as if she had not seen them before. Then she said:

"Very well. I will send Aldora in here to talk to you, but she is a strange girl and I do not pretend to understand her. However I cannot believe that with your proverbial charm, dear Ingram, any woman, young or old, would refuse you anything!"

She was deliberately flattering him, but in fact, she was also being quite sincere.

The Duke had the uncomfortable feeling that the Marchioness did not only not understand her daughter, but did not know her at all well.

She rose to her feet.

"I need not add," she said, "what a pleasure it will be to have you as my son-in-law and also to see you in a position in which I know you will excel."

She gave a very sweet smile as she added:

"India's gain will be our loss, for we shall miss you very

much. However in five years you may be able to do more for our great Empire of which we are so proud than any one man has ever done before."

It was a very pretty speech and the Duke appreciated it.

Moving towards the Marchioness he took her hand and raised it to his lips.

"You have always been very kind to me," he said, "and perhaps the only compensation for surrendering my bachelorhood will be that I shall be related to you!"

The Marchioness smiled.

"Thank you, Ingram," she said, "and it is something I shall enjoy tremendously!"

She did not say any more but went from the room and the Duke returned to the window to stand looking out again into the night.

He knew that India had been dangled in front of his eyes like a glittering bauble.

At the same time, because he was so well read and made himself *au fait* with everything that was happening in the Empire, he knew there were dozens of problems for which he would have to find a solution.

But especially there was the one to which the Marchioness had referred and which had been handled in such a disastrous fashion by Lord Northbrook two years earlier.

What it amounted to was that Sher Ali, one of the many sons of the previous ruler, had won for himself, with no help from the British, an uneasy throne as Amir of Khabul, the Capital of Afghanistan.

The Afghans were a proud and independent people, and Sher Ali did not want to have anything to do with either Russia or England, both of whom were maneouvring secretly to extend their influence over his country.

When the Russians crept closer and became more menacing Sher Ali thought he would be wise to place himself under the protection of one or other of the great powers.

He trusted the British more than the Russians and he sent a special envoy to Lord Northbrook and offered him a Treaty by which in return for his allegiance to the British they would guarantee him money, and recognise his favourite younger son as his heir, and would additionally in the event of a Russian invasion, come to his assistance.

Gladstone's Government however instructed Lord Northbrook to refuse the suggestion and to berate Sher Ali for trying to disinherit his elder son.

This made Sher Ali immediately favour the Russians.

The Duke was aware that the moment Mr. Disraeli became Prime Minister he was extremely perturbed about this error of judgment which was certain eventually to cost a great number of British lives on the treacherous and dangerous North-West Frontier.

Everything the Duke had read about the situation now came flooding back into his mind, and he found himself thinking how he would handle Sher Ali in the future, and how diplomatic overtures towards him should start immediately.

He was so deeply involved in thinking out what was the best approach that it was quite a shock when the Sitting-Room door opened and Aldora came in.

He saw by the expression on her face and the fury in her eyes what he was to expect.

As she shut the door behind her, she did not wait for the Duke to speak but walked towards him saying:

"Why am I sent to you, or need I ask? Have you told Mama that you have no intention of marrying me?"

The question seemed to ring out in the room and the Duke replied:

"I want to talk to you, Aldora."

"There is nothing to talk about. I have told you I hate and despise you! I loathe the way you behave with women and I would rather die than marry you!"

"Do not be so dramatic!" the Duke said sharply. "I want

to tell you what has been suggested. I think it will interest you."

"Nothing interests me which concerns you!" Aldora retorted. "I know without your telling me that you have agreed to Mama's suggestion and that you expect me to recognise what an advantage it would be for me to be your wife. But let me make it quite clear – I will not marry you, not if you drag me screaming to the altar!"

"For goodness sake!" the Duke exclaimed. "Let me tell you what your mother has said to me, and let us discuss this rationally."

"There is nothing to discuss – nothing to talk about!" Aldora replied. "I hate you and the sooner you get that into your head the better!"

As she spoke, almost spitting the words at him, she ran past him out into the garden.

For a moment he saw her gown silhouetted against the shadows and the moonlight was silver on her hair.

Then she had disappeared and the Duke was alone.

He would not think what he could do, or how he could cope with the situation.

Then he knew, and the fact infuriated him, that he was powerless.

"The Marchioness will have to talk to her own daughter!" he told himself. "She certainly has no intention of listening to me!"

He finished his brandy, then went slowly back through the Drawing-Room where everybody was playing cards.

The Marchioness was talking to one of her guests but was obviously worried.

As the Duke came through the door she looked at him, and because he knew there was a question in her eyes he shook his head.

He saw her frown and knew she understood, and in her usual tactful way arranged for him to take a seat at the table where the previous player wished to leave because he had a long way to go before he reached home.

It was an hour later before the party broke up and everybody had said goodbye to their hostess.

The Duke was the last, and she asked him in a low voice:

"What happened?"

"Your daughter would not listen to me!" the Duke replied. "I think in fact, you were aware before I arrived that she has what seems to be an unreasonable dislike of me."

The Marchioness sighed.

"I was rather afraid of that."

"Well, there is nothing I can do," the Duke said in a tone of exasperation. "Perhaps you could talk to her and make her see sense."

"I will certainly try," the Marchioness replied, "but I do find my daughters very much more difficult than my son."

She walked across the hall and up the stairs and the Duke went to the Library to collect a newspaper to read in bed before he followed her.

He was in fact in bed and holding the newspaper in his hand, even though he was thinking of India, when there came a knock at his door.

The Duke was surprised because he was just beginning to feel sleepy, despite the fact that he had so much to think about.

Two nights with Fenella, followed by morning rides and long days of racing had begun to take their toll.

Automatically he called: "Come in!" and the door opened and to his astonishment the Marchioness stood there.

She came into the room and shut the door behind her.

As he stared at her realising she was wearing a negligee and her hair was covered by a little lace cap, she said:

"Aldora has run away, and I do not know what to do about it!"

The Duke sat up in bed.

"Run away?" he asked. "What do you mean?"

The Marchioness sat down on a nearby chair.

"When I went to bed," she said, "I lay thinking about Aldora and decided it would be best if I spoke to her at once. I therefore went to her room to find that she had changed from her evening-gown which was lying on the floor and I am certain put on her riding-habit."

She paused, then went on:

"As I was wondering what I should do I saw a note, which I had not noticed before, on her pillow and I have brought it to show you."

She opened the piece of paper and read aloud:

"I will not marry that abominable man as I have already told him. I have therefore gone away and you will not be able to find me, so do not try.

Aldora."

The Marchioness's voice faltered as she read the last word, then looking at the Duke in desperation asked:

"Where can she have gone? What can we do?"

What Aldora had said to him the first time they had spoken came into his mind.

"It is possible," he said after a moment, "that she will try to get to France."

"To France?" the Marchioness exclaimed. "But she knows nobody there. What will happen to her? We must somehow stop her!"

The Duke knew it was not going to be easy and the Marchioness went on as if she was speaking to herself.

"Think of the scandal if the newspapers get hold of it especially if they discover the reason she has left in such a precipitate fashion!"

The Duke knew the Marchioness was suggesting that it would involve him.

He could think of nothing more degrading than that a young girl of eighteen should run away from him because she was afraid that she might have to marry him.

"Who is aware of what you have said to me tonight?" he asked.

The Marchioness looked uncomfortable.

"I have not of course, said anything about India because the Queen swore me to secrecy."

"But you have said that I might marry Aldora!"

"I only mentioned it to one or two of my closest friends.

The Duke thought grimly that this meant it would be common knowledge in Court circles and anywhere else where the gossips' tongues never stopped wagging.

He thought for a moment, then he said:

"The only thing I can do, and I shall have to hurry, is to try to prevent Aldora from boarding a ship for France. I suppose your closest port is Chichester harbour."

"That is the nearest," the Marchioness agreed, "and I imagine there will be ships sailing across the Channel from there."

"As it happens my own yacht is in the harbour," the Duke said, "because I was thinking I might spend a few days on her after I leave here."

"If Aldora has already crossed the Channel you will never find her!"

"I can but try," the Duke replied, "but France is a very large country!"

"Then hurry, please hurry!" the Marchioness begged urgently. "The child has no idea of the danger she is in if she travels about alone."

Then she said:

"I blame myself for not explaining it to her better, but I thought you would do that!"

The Duke felt there was not point in saying that Aldora had prevented him from saying anything and he merely replied:

"If I am to catch her I must leave at once."

"Yes, of course, and please, please bring her safely back without anybody else being aware of what has occurred."

"I shall certainly do my best!" the Duke replied.

The Marchioness went from the room, and throwing off the bedclothes the Duke pulled violently at the bell beside the bed two or three times before he started hastily to dress himself.

CHAPTER FOUR

The Duke went to the stables and found as he expected that the only sounds were those of the horses moving in their stalls and everybody else was asleep.

He was aware that the stable boys would be in the attic overhead while the Head Groom doubtless had a cottage or better accommodation elsewhere.

He therefore shouted up the narrow stairs which led to the attic and a few minutes later one of his own stable boys came hurrying down the stairs pulling on his trousers.

"I want *Samson* saddled immediately," the Duke said and walked towards the stallion's stall.

It took nearly five minutes before *Samson* was saddled and bridled while the Duke was aware that Aldora was, every second, getting further and further away from him.

Just before he mounted he said to the boy:

"I believe Her Ladyship has gone riding. How long ago did she leave?"

The boy hesitated for a moment before he replied:

"Oi didn't know it were 'Er Ladyship, Yer Grace, but Oi 'ears somebody takin' a 'orse out into th' yard."

"How long ago?" the Duke repeated impatiently.

"Oi should say 'bout twenty minutes to 'alf an hour, Yer Grace."

The Duke swung himself into the saddle and moved off.

It was fortunate that he had not ridden *Samson* that morning, but one of the other horses, so that the stallion was fresh and ready for anything that was required of him.

Having stayed so many times at Goodwood House the

Duke knew the surrounding countryside almost as well as he knew his own land in Buckinghamshire.

As soon as he had cleared the Park he set off across country, heading due South towards Chichester Harbour.

As he went he thought that, if Aldora did not find a ship sailing at dawn for France, she would probably go on to Portsmouth where there would be ships sailing regularly back and forth across the Channel.

Although he knew Chichester Harbour well, he had never particularly noticed what type of ships put in there, being more concerned with the private yachts like his own.

He had found it an excellent and quiet harbour near to several houses in which he so often stayed.

As he had told the Marchioness, he had planned, since the London Season was finished, to take the opportunity after Goodwood to spend a few days or perhaps longer aboard his new yacht.

It had only just been delivered from the Ship Builders and was the very latest type of steam yacht yet produced.

He was aware that, as his horses were, it would be the envy and admiration of all his friends, and he was looking forward to showing it to them, but was determined first to test out for himself all the innovations it incorporated.

It seemed to him extremely inappropriate and annoying that it should be used for the first time in chasing a tiresome young woman across the Channel.

As he had thought before, she should have been better disciplined by her mother and by her father when he was still alive, and it was because she had been abominably spoilt that Aldora was causing him so much trouble and anxiety.

It also infuriated him to learn that the Marchioness had discussed his private affairs with her friends.

He knew, because the Queen was so powerful, that it would be very difficult for any man whatever his position in life to refuse a marriage which carried with it the promise of such a glittering reward.

"If I had any sense," the Duke told himself, "I would go to see the Queen, explain to her how it is totally impossible for me to marry Aldora, and promise to find myself a more suitable wife in the least possible time."

Then he had the uncomfortable feeling that the Queen would not listen to him, having no idea what Aldora was really like.

"Her Majesty will have been fed with tales of her clever brain and her intellectual achievements," he told himself scornfully, "and will not understand that she is really an obnoxious brat who behaves in a quite unprecedented manner."

At the same time he was forced to acknowledge what a good story it would make for the gossips, if they ever found out, that a mere school girl had taken him to task for his amatory behaviour and that she had then run away from the prospect of such a disreputable bridegroom would lose nothing in the telling.

At the onset, nobody was likely to believe so unlikely a story.

Nevertheless they would repeat it, mull over it, and laugh about it. It would grow and grow and the Duke knew if he walked into White's or any of his other Clubs he would be aware what they were saying about him.

"Dammit!" he swore aloud. "I will make her my wife, if only to show that she cannot ride rough-shod over me!"

Then he was astounded at what he had just said.

Could it be true that the Duke of Wydeminster, who was noted for his fastidiousness where women were concerned and who was pursued by almost every Beauty in the Social World, was really contemplating marrying a young hooligan who had declared she would rather die than marry him?

"I must be getting as mental as she is!" the Duke exclaimed savagely.

He spurred *Samson* as he spoke to go faster.

It was fortunate there was a moon to show him the way and as he was familiar with the ground over which he was travelling he made good progress.

Every minute the smell of the sea seemed to be getting stronger and he thought it would not be long before he could see it.

Then he thought he could hear thunder and a quarter-of-an-hour later was aware of a sensational change in the weather.

The claps of thunder were rapidly growing nearer and as flashes of fork lightning lit up the surrounding countryside the rain began to pour down.

The Duke was aware that he was going to get very wet.

But what was more disturbing was that *Samson* disliked thunder and started to rear at every crash. Then as the rain became torrential he slowed his pace and made every effort not to proceed any further.

The Duke knew that this part of Sussex was notorious for occasional storms of quite frightening severity.

On one occasion the spire of Chichester Cathedral had been struck by lightning and the top forty feet of it destroyed.

On another the whole spire had collapsed in a heavy gale.

The Duke remembered being told about it five years later when he was staying with the Duke of Richmond.

It had been a tragic and extremely dramatic accident when the spire had simply disappeared falling precipitously into the body of the building.

The Duke had been staying at Goodwood, having just come down from Oxford, when in 1865 the Duke of Richmond had laid the foundation stone of yet another spire.

Now the weather was growing more tempestuous and he wondered if it would survive tonight's treatment.

By now the fork lightning and another violent clap of thunder directly overhead made him aware that *Samson* could go no further.

He was wondering what he cold do when he saw just ahead of him the roofs of a house and decided, however strange it might be to call in the middle of the night, that he must seek shelter.

With some difficulty he rode *Samson* towards the building and found when he reached it that it was an Inn.

There was a court-yard in which another flash of lightning revealed some ramshackle stables.

Whatever they were like, he knew *Samson* would be glad of their protection.

He dismounted, opened the rickety door and led the horse inside.

The stables smelt foul, and he suspected that not only were they as delapidated inside as they were out, but they were also dirty.

The lightning coming through the broken panes of a window showed him there was a row of stalls and the one opposite him was empty, while next to it there was another horse.

He put *Samson* inside and saw again in the next flash that there was hay in the manger and a bucket containing water.

He pulled off the stallion's bridle but did not touch the saddle, hoping that with any luck the storm would soon be over and he would be able to proceed in his pursuit of Aldora.

He shut the door of the stall, hung the bridle on a hook protruding from the wall, and walked through the rain that was still pouring relentlessly, to the door of the Inn.

There were lights in the windows and he imagined there was another traveller like himself who had found it impossible to go any further.

He opened the door, taking off his hat as he did so, and a cascade of water fell from it onto the ground.

Then he saw with a sense of relief there was a large fire burning in an open fireplace facing him.

He moved towards it and then saw there was somebody sitting in an arm-chair which had its back to the door.

He could see the golden hair of the occupier's head and knew that by a stroke of incredibly good fortune he had found Aldora!

She was obviously not interested in learning who had just come in out of the rain.

Only when he reached the hearth rug to turn his back to the fire did he see her start at the sight of him while her hands clutched the arms of her chair.

"I expect," the Duke said, brushing his wet hair back from his forehead, "that your horse dislikes the storm as much as *Samson* does. I only got him into the stable with the greatest of difficulty."

He spoke in a normal, conversational tone as if they were at Berkhampton House.

"Why are you . . . here?" Aldora demanded.

The Duke put his hat on the floor and began to unbutton his coat.

"Before we start fighting again," he said, "would you mind if I take off my coat and dry it in front of the fire? I have a strong dislike of catching cold, an affliction which I am quite certain threatens us both."

He saw as he spoke that Aldora's riding jacket was arranged over a chair on one side of the fireplace, and as it was steaming he knew she was as wet as he was.

She did not answer and he removed his coat, finding the rain had seeped through the fine whipcord and that the shoulders of his white lawn shirt also were wet.

He hung his coat over a chair on the opposite side of the fireplace from Aldora's.

As it began to steam he asked:

"Is there any chance of anything to drink in this place?"

As he spoke he looked around and knew it was the type of Inn which neither Aldora nor he would, in normal circumstances, have entered in a thousand years.

The ceiling had heavy ship's timbers across it, the floor was flagged and undoubtedly dirty, while a few tattered rugs were probably dirtier still.

There were several wooden arm-chairs and some others with wicker seats which all needed repairing. Altogether it was a very unpreposessing sight.

As if in answer to his question, through the door underneath some stairs came a large man who was obviously the Inn-keeper.

He was as dirty as his surroundings and he must have dressed, perhaps when Aldora arrived, in a hurry, for his shirt was open at the neck and his breeches undone at the knees.

It was obvious as he advanced towards them that he was impressed by the Duke's appearance, and in his soft Sussex accent he asked:

"Be there anythin' I can get ye, Sir?"

Before the Duke could reply, Aldora to his surprise said in French so that the Inn-keeper would not understand:

"I am sure the only thing which would not poison you is the brandy, on which our host is very unlikely to have paid any Customs Duty!"

The Duke found himself smiling at what she had said, and as the Inn-keeper was waiting enquiringly, he replied:

"I would like a glass of brandy, if you have some, but bring me the bottle."

He knew as he spoke that unless he saw the bottle anything he was given in a glass was likely to be of inferior quality or, as Aldora had said, what amounted to poison.

"Oi'll get it fer ye, Sir," the Inn-keeper replied.

As he walked away the Duke saw that by Aldora's side was a small wooden stool on which stood a glass.

"Is that brandy you are drinking?" he asked.

"Yes, and it is quite palatable, although I did not think of asking to see the bottle," she replied, "but I shall remember that another time."

The Duke who could feel the warmth from the fire drying his breeches which had become soaked asked sharply:

"Must there be another time? I am finding travelling in this weather exceedingly unpleasant!"

"You can hardly expect me to apologise for the storm!"

She paused, then added:

"I am surprised you found out so quickly that I had left."

"Your mother went to your bedroom to speak to you."

Aldora raised her eyebrows.

"That is strange! I have never known her before not to wait until the morning to rebuke me."

"She considered this rather serious."

"Why is it so serious?"

"Because for you to disappear would undoubtedly cause a scandal for you, and make me, as you had threatened, a laughing stock."

There was silence for a moment. Then Aldora said:

"I had not thought that my leaving home before there was any talk of our being . . . married would affect . . . you."

The Duke was just about to reply when the Inn-keeper came back with a bottle in his hand and a glass on a broken wooden tray.

One glance at the bottle told the Duke that Aldora was right: it had undoubtedly been smuggled in from France without the Coast-Guards being aware of it.

Smuggling had become a national pastime during the Napoleonic wars, and it was still very common along the South Coast of England.

Although the Coast-Guards tried, it was impossible for them to keep a successful watch along so many miles of small bays, harbours and mouths of rivers.

The Duke took the glass from the tray and the bottle from the Inn-keeper's hand.

"That'll cost ye a guinea, Sir," the man said apprehensively.

It was an exorbitant charge and the Duke new it, but he merely drew a loose guinea from his waistcoat pocket and threw it on to the wooden tray.

Almost as if he was afraid he would take it back again the Inn-keeper hurried away.

The cork of the bottle had already been drawn, but it was pressed back into the neck, and the Duke saw that a small amount of brandy had been removed which he supposed was what Aldora was now drinking.

"Let me fill your glass," he suggested.

"I do not wish to be so drunk that I am unable to continue with my ride," Aldora said provocatively.

"I think that might be better than having streaming eyes and a running nose."

As if his answer was somewhat unexpected she gave a little chuckle.

He poured some more brandy into her glass and filled his own, then sat down in a chair beside her facing the fire.

"This is certainly more comfortable than braving the elements," he said, "which I find decidedly hostile."

He knew as he spoke that she was surprised. Then after a moment she said a little hesitatingly:

"You . . . cannot force me to . . . return with you!"

"I admit it might be rather difficult," the Duke replied, "unless, and you have put the thought into my head, I make you so drunk that I can carry you back unconscious."

She laughed and it was a pretty sound.

"I think that would be too sensational and would certainly cause a remarkable deal of gossip!"

She chuckled again before she said:

"'*Duke Captures Runaway Heiress And Carries Her Unconscious Across His Saddle To Be Reunited With Her Weeping Mother!*'"

She glanced at the Duke to see the result of her mockery, then asked:

"I do not suppose Mama was weeping?"

"No, only extremely worried about what the Queen would say if she learned of your behaviour."

"The Queen? What has the Queen to do with it?"

"It was Her Majesty who suggested I should marry you," the Duke said quietly.

Aldora stared at him in silence. Then she exclaimed:

"I can hardly believe that Mama really asked the Queen to find me a husband!"

"That would not be altogether extratordinary since you are her God-child."

He was silent for some seconds before he added:

"Actually, you merely fitted in with the plans she has for me."

"For you?" Aldora repeated curiously.

"She is thinking of appointing me Viceroy of India!"

Again there was silence and Aldora stared at him in obvious astonishment before she said:

"I cannot see that that has anything to do with me."

"A Viceroy is expected to be married."

"And you will be Viceroy of India?"

"Only if you consent to marry me. Otherwise Her Majesty will appoint somebody in my place."

"I do not believe it! Your are just making this up!"

"I swear to you it is the truth, at least it is what your mother told me, and what I had intended to tell you tonight, if only you had listened."

Aldora drew in her breath, then she exclaimed:

"I have never heard of anything so monstrous that Mama should aspire to my being the wife of the Viceroy! She would not understand what it meant!"

"Your mother is an extremely intelligent woman, as everybody is aware," the Duke said, "so I do not think it particularly surprising that she should be ambitious for you."

"No, that is true," Aldora conceded. "She managed to get a Prince for Mary, and a rich Earl for Phoebe, but I should not have thought she had the imagination to think of the Viceroy for me!"

"I think we can attribute that idea entirely to the Queen."

The Duke poured himself a little more brandy and thought that it had taken away the chill of his damp clothes.

It had also swept away some of the irritation he felt at having to get out of bed and chase this ridiculous young woman in a storm which was still raging over-dramatically outside.

"I am just wondering," Aldora said reflectively, "whether Mama has been very, very clever, or whether it is fate that you should be offered the position of Viceroy with me thrown in as part of the package."

Because the Duke thought once again that she was being rude he merely replied sharply:

"I should have thought after all this talk of your powers of perception, or 'Eye' as you like to call it, you would know the answer to that!"

"It is very difficult to be clairvoyant about one's self," Aldora answered, "but where India is concerned, that is something very different."

"Why?"

"Because it is the one place I have always wanted to go, the one place where everything that has inspired me, everything I have found interesting, has originated."

She spoke in a dreamy voice that was quite different from the usually aggressive way in which she addressed him.

The Duke asked quietly:

"Are you referring to the religions of India? To Buddhism, for example?"

"Of course," Aldora replied. "Buddhism and the Vedas, the secret writings that are hidden away in Temples and Palaces and in the hearts of those strange, unpredictable people whom their conquerors do not begin to understand."

"That is a little sweeping," the Duke persisted. "I think a

great number of people have tried to understand such secrets, and have partially succeeded."

"That is what Papa thought," Aldora said, "but most people who have visited India, the Statesmen who talk about it, and those like Lord Northbrook who govern it, have not the slightest idea of what the Indians themselves think and believe, and the gods they have worshipped since the beginning of time."

She spoke so passionately that the Duke turned his head and looked at her in surprise.

"I have always told myself," Aldora went on, as if she was speaking to somebody else rather than the man sitting beside her, "that one day I would go to India, and that is why I am studying Urdu and some of the other languages, and finding them completely enthralling."

The Duke understood now the conversation he had been so surprised to overhear between her and the Ambassador.

Yet for a moment he could hardly credit she was not putting on an act to impress him.

There was silence. Then after a moment he said:

"If what you tell me is true, here is your opportunity perhaps sent by fate, or by your Karma for you to see India as no other woman of your age is ever likely to do."

"In your . . . company!"

The inference in her voice was very obvious.

"As you say, in my company," the Duke agreed.

As he took another sip of brandy he said:

"Because for the moment we are sitting in a kind of 'No-man's-land', and there is, through sheer force of circumstances a kind of Armistice between us, perhaps you will tell me why you dislike me to the extent that you are prepared to run away from everything that is safe and familiar, to what, if you think it over, must be a very frightening future."

"I can manage on my own," Aldora replied defiantly.

"I doubt it," the Duke said, "but I do not want to argue

with you. I just want to understand your reasons for attempting to live a life that to any other woman would seem terrifyingly dangerous."

"That is something I have no intention of telling you."

"I could understand that, if we were still sitting comfortably in your home," the Duke said. "But because there is nobody here to interrupt us or overhear what we might say, surely you could stretch a point and pander to my curiosity?"

"You will not like what I tell you!"

"That is a risk I am prepared to take."

"Very well," Aldora said.

She took another sip from her glass as if she felt it gave her courage. Then after a pause she said:

"I will tell you first about myself."

"I am anxious to learn everything," the Duke said, "however unpleasant!"

He thought she smiled as if she had made him apprehensive of what he might learn. Then she began:

"Mama has always been extremely ambitious for my sisters and me socially. But Papa was different."

There was a note in her voice that told the Duke that her father had meant very much more to her than her mother did.

Not wishing to interrupt but rather to prompt her he remarked:

"I gather you were very fond of your father."

"I love him," Aldora said simply. "It was Papa who, because he was disappointed I was not a boy, taught me to think, to learn and to know that knowledge is the only thing that is never disappointing."

The Duke began to understand how everybody who spoke about Aldora said how clever she was.

"But Papa is dead," she went on, "and Mama is determined that I shall hold a brilliant social position like my sisters."

Her voice sharpened as she said:

"Mary was forced to marry Prince Frederick of Guttenberg even though she loathed the sight of him. He is pompous, stupid and completely convinced that women are inferior creatures to be dominated by men."

Aldora drew in her breath.

"Mary is utterly miserable and imprisoned in a marriage from which she can never escape."

"I cannot believe," the Duke remarked, thinking of how much he had always admired the Marchioness, "that your mother meant that to happen."

"Of course not," Aldora agreed, "but Prince Frederick proposed, and how could she refuse when Mary would be a ruling Princess, even though Guttenburg is a small, unpleasant, backward State under the heel of Prussia?"

The Duke had no answer to this, and he merely waited until Aldora continued:

"Phoebe was in love with a young man she had known all her life. He was a Country Squire, but he was not good enough for Mama. My sister was told to marry the extremely wealthy Earl of Fenwick who possessed huge estates and held a title that had been conferred on his ancestor in the 13th Century."

Again there was a note of almost painful bitterness in Aldora's voice as she said:

"He is a hopeless drunkard, but not so drunk as to be incapable of knocking Phoebe about, and using the most appalling language to her."

The Duke stared at Aldora as if he could hardly believe what she was saying.

He was seeing in his mind's eye, at Buckingham Palace a year ago the white drawn face of the Princess Frederick of Guttenburg, and remembering how he had thought at the time she looked ill and unhappy.

He had heard tales of the Earl of Fenwick's behaviour and of how he had been blackballed from several Clubs.

But it was still hard for him to believe that the Marchioness had really forced her daughters to accept such undesirable husbands.

And yet he knew if he was honest that in the Social World in which he moved few girls had any choice as to whom they married.

When they emerged from the School-Room, it was accepted that the sooner their parents arranged for them to be taken up the aisle the better.

It was also taken for granted that the greater the matrimonial catch, the more admirable the maternal instinct had been.

"I can only say," he said aloud, "that your sisters have been very unfortunate, and I can understand that you have no wish to emulate them."

Aldora made a little movement with her head as though she acknowledge he was accepting what she had told him. Then she said:

"And now, as you are so keen to know the truth, I will tell you why I have no intention of marrying you."

"I am listening," the Duke said gravely.

"You may have forgotten her, but three years ago Lady Lawson came to stay at Berkhampton House, *after she had been ill.*"

The Duke was suddenly rigid.

He recognised the name – of course he did! And there was no need for Aldora to have stressed the words: *'after she had been ill'*.

Eleinor Lawson had, after he had left her, cried herself into a state which the Doctors could only describe as one of nervous frustration.

It was of course something he had never meant to happen and he admitted to himself soon after he had become entangled with Eleinor that he had made a grave mistake.

She was very beautiful, and at twenty-five years of age she had attained polish and poise and due to her husband's importance she glittered in the Social World like an evening star.

Lord Lawson was a Gentleman-in-Waiting to the Queen, a man of dignity and considerable presence, besides being wealthy and in his time an extremely distinguished soldier.

He had married when he was over fifty a young girl with no experience of life, but whose beauty was undeniable and by whom, like many old men before him, he was completely captivated.

Although her parents were of indisputable lineage they were poor, and they had been delighted when Eleinor was swept off her feet.

She was married before she had the least idea what it would entail, or what living with a husband almost old enough to be her grandfather would be like.

At first her position, the beautiful clothes she could now afford, and the presents that her husband gave her made her feel as if she was living in a fairy-story.

Then as Lord Lawson, very set in his ways, expected his wife to be obedient to his every wish and conform to his old-fashioned and unbending ideas, Eleinor became restive.

It did not take her long to realise the power of her beauty, and as most men were interested in that only, they had no idea how little intelligence or commonsense she had.

The Duke was not Eleinor's first lover, but he was unfortunately the one with whom she fell in love. And she did this not simply in the way that other Beauties loved him – admiringly, adoring, and for them whole-heartedly.

For Eleinor it was a traumatic experience that swept her into the sky and she ceased to think of anything or care about anything but her love.

It was all-consuming, and was, the Duke found, frightening in its intensity.

As usual he had never expected to become so involved or indeed to hurt anybody until he realised too late how over emotional she was, almost to the point of insanity.

He pleaded with her to show discretion, to be affectionate towards her husband, and above all not to parade her emotions in public.

He might have been talking to a stone wall.

Eleinor enveloped him, clung to him, suffocated him with her love, until he knew there was only one thing to do, and that was to cut her completely out of his life.

He had to do something to forestal a scandal which would rock Society, upset the Court, and inevitably destroy her.

He had thought her beautiful, which she undoubtedly was, but long before he made love to her she had thrown herself into his arms and more or less forced him to become her lover.

When he left her, making it quite clear that for both their sakes they must separate, she had been just as unrestrained at losing him as she had been in showing her affection before he was ready for it.

He learned that her unhappiness had made her ill.

While he was genuinely sorry he had been instrumental in causing it, to have written to her or sent her flowers would only have prolonged the agony.

He could only withdraw completely, taking care that he did not meet her by chance at any party, and avoiding mutual friends who might misguidedly have tried to bring them together again.

He had heard that Eleinor had retired to the country, but what he had not learned was that it was to Berkhampton House.

"She told me," Aldora was saying, "how much she had loved you and how cruel you had been in saying you would not see her any more. She cried and cried!"

The pain in Aldora's voice was very obvious, and the Duke thought that only an unstable woman like Eleinor would have confided in a girl of fifteen.

He knew that at that age, knowing nothing about love personally, she would have been very vulnerable and an older woman's unhappiness would effect her deeply.

"I tried to help her," Aldora murmured, "but she only cried and said you had taken her heart from her and all she wanted to do was to . . . die!"

The Duke's lips tightened.

Eleinor had not died. In fact she had returned to her husband had he happened to know she had subsequently had several love-affairs.

She had certainly not been as dramatic about them as she had where he was concerned, and none of her lovers had lasted for long.

The last time the Duke had heard of her she was in Paris behaving somewhat blatantly with a French *Marquis* who, according to the Duke's informant, had covered her with diamonds which even rivalled those of the Parisian Courtesans.

He was tempted to defend himself by telling Aldora all this, but he felt she would not believe him and might only hate him all the more.

"When I listened to Lady Lawson," she was saying, "I swore I would never let that happen to me! But of course, I never anticipated for one moment that Mama would choose . . . you as my . . . husband!"

The Duke was silent for a moment. Then he said:

"Perhaps a Yogi, if you consulted one, would tell you it is fate. Our lives are eternally intermingled, and if we hurt someone that is a debt which we carry with us to our next existence and which eventually must be paid."

He knew as he spoke, looking at the fire as he did so, that Aldora had turned to stare at him, her eyes very wide, an expression of surprise in them.

Then she asked:

"Why should . . . you think that? Why should you say such . . . things?"

"Because I suppose it is the only explanation I can offer," the Duke replied.

Almost as if he had frightened her, Aldora got up from her chair and walked across the room to the door.

For a moment the Duke wondered if she was going to run away from him as she had done from Berkhampton House.

Then as she stood in the open doorway she said:

"The rain has stopped and the sky is clearing."

"In which case," the Duke replied, "we can be on our way."

Aldora shut the door.

He stood with his back to the fire facing her as she came towards him, and he knew before she spoke that she was asking him a question.

She reached him, then tipped back her head to look up at him.

There was a long pause.

"Very well," she said at length. "You have found me and I will come back with you. But I do not intend to marry you and I am sure we can find some way by which you can become the Viceroy of India without me."

"I doubt it," the Duke said dryly. "In fact I was convinced from the way your mother spoke that you really are part of the deal."

There was silence before she asked:

"Do you really think Mama can . . . force me into . . . marrying you?"

"Only if I am to be Viceroy of India!"

Again they were both silent until Aldora said:

"Would you mind . . . very much if you had to . . . refuse?"

"I do not think it is a question of my refusing the position," the Duke answered. "What the Queen and your mother have concocted between them is, that if our engagement is announced I shall be approached by the India Office."

His voice was slightly mocking as he went on:

"I suppose most men would jump at the idea of being

Viceroy, so I do not expect I can prevaricate for more than a few days."

He smiled a little wryly before he corrected his last words by saying:

"It is actually a case of awaiting your decision, not mine!"

Unexpectedly Aldora stamped her foot.

"It is extremely unfair and typical of Mama!" she said. "If only Papa were alive, he would not allow her to behave in such a way!"

Her voice softened as she went on:

"He was deeply distressed that Mary and Phoebe were so unhappy, and he always said to me: 'That shall never happen to you, my dearest. You must marry for love, or remain with me!'"

"Your father was right," the Duke said quietly.

"I know, and there is .. nobody I love."

She made it sound a challenge, as if she defied the Duke even to think of love where he was concerned.

Then he began tentatively:

"Suppose . . . ?"

"No!" Aldora interrupted. "No, no, no! I am well aware of what you are going to say, and the answer is 'No!' Why should I care whether you are the Viceroy or the Sultan of Zanzibar? You are nothing in my life and I wish, when the races are over, never to see you again!"

"Very well," the Duke said. "If that is your final decision there is no point in our going on talking about it. And now, I suppose, as it must be very nearly dawn we should return home and have a few hours' sleep before we watch my horse win the Goodwood Cup!"

Aldora gave a little laugh.

"I should not be too sure!" she said. "My 'Eye' may find an outsider who will romp home."

"In which case," the Duke said, "I shall see that you are tested on the ducking-stool as a witch for putting a spell on me!"

Aldora laughed again.

"I might even do that!" she threatened.

She did not wait for the Duke's answer, but walked out into the courtyard towards the stables.

CHAPTER FIVE

By the time they had saddled Aldora's horse, put a bridle on *Samson*, and came out into the court-yard, dawn had broken.

Now the first pale fingers of the sun were sweeping away the last sable of the night, and because of the rain the whole world smelled fresh and fragrant.

The Duke lifted Aldora into the saddle, then mounted his own horse.

There had been no sign of the Proprietor and the Duke suspected he had retired to bed, so he left a guinea on the table just inside the door.

It was gross over-payment for what they had received in the dirty Inn, but he was grateful that he had found Aldora and did not have to go any further in search of her.

At the same time, as they rode away the Duke was regretting that he could not go to India.

He knew that in the circumstances there would be no point in his even discussing it with the Queen or the India Office.

He thought a little wryly as they rode along the road that it was the first time in his life that a woman had prevented him from doing what he wanted.

It was also the first time a woman had hated him with a violence which had blinded her to everything but what she thought of as his depravity.

The road was wet and muddy from the storm, and the Duke said as they proceeded:

"Although it may be rather hard going I think we should

go back the way I came, which was across the fields."

"Of course," Aldora agreed.

They looked for a gap in the hedgerows by which they could leave the road and a short distance later came upon a small wood where because the trees grew right down to the roadside there was a break in the hedges.

Aldora turned her horse up what appeared to be a rough cart-track and then, as the Duke followed her, stopped to let him go ahead.

There was not room for them to ride abreast until they came to a clearing where it was obvious a number of trees had been cut down.

The wood ahead looked thick and without a track in it, and the Duke paused for a few moments, wondering if it would be best to turn to the right and force their way through the trees onto what he was sure would be open fields beyond.

He was just about to ask Aldora what she thought, when a hoarse, common voice ejaculated:

"Put yer 'ands up! Oi've got yer covered!"

Both Aldora and the Duke looked in astonishment at the man who had come riding through the thick trees ahead of them.

For a moment it seemed incredible that he actually had a pistol in his hand which was pointing at the Duke.

He was wearing a mask over his face, and was very roughly dressed with a tattered handkerchief round his neck, and a worn felt hat pulled low over his eyes.

He was unshaven, his coat was ragged, and his horse old and ungroomed, the bridle mended with pieces of string.

"If you are holding me up for the money I have on me," the Duke remarked calmly, "then you are unfortunate."

"Oi'll tak' yer money an' Oi'll tak' yer 'orse!" the man said aggressively.

The way he spoke, and the pistol he held in an unexpectedly steady hand pointing at his chest, made the

Duke aware that the Highwayman, if that was what he was, was definitely dangerous.

Too late he realised that he had been very foolish in riding after Aldora without remembering that in race-week there was always a great number of thieves, robbers, footpads and tricksters of every sort and description waiting to extort money from the race-goers.

When he was driving he invariably had a pistol with him in the vehicle in which he was travelling, just in case he was waylaid by the type of individual who was facing him now.

As it happened, it was such a long time since he had encountered anything so disagreeable that he had almost forgotten the necessity for such a precaution.

Now he realised that he was in a very uncomfortable situation, and although he did not think the man would actually kill him he began to wonder desperately how he could prevent him from taking *Samson*.

He could imagine nothing more humiliating than being deprived like this of one of his best stallions, and what was more it would be intolerable for a horse as fine as *Samson*.

He had a deep affection for the animal and it was unthinkable that any horse he owned should come into the possession of anybody as unpleasant as the man now threatening him.

One look at the Highwayman's face was enough to tell the Duke he could be cruel if it suited him, and the horse he was riding had obviously been neglected, if not badly treated for many years.

"Let us discuss this sensibly," the Duke said in a calm voice.

"There ain't nothin' ter discuss, Mister," the Highwayman replied aggressively. "Just yer get down off yer 'orse an' be quick abaht it, or yer'll find dead men don't ride!"

He almost snarled the last words and the Duke was aware that never in his whole life had he been in quite such a dangerous situation.

He realised the Highwayman had his finger on the trigger and knew now with an instinct that could not be denied that he did intend to kill him.

Then suddenly there was an explosion that seemed almost to break his eardrums.

The Highwayman made a gutteral sound in his throat before his whole body swayed backwards and he fell from his saddle to the ground.

He must however have pulled the trigger of his own pistol a split second after Aldora shot him for as he fell there was another explosion and the Duke felt the impact as if of a red-hot bullet on the outside of his left arm.

It did not knock him over and he sat firm in his saddle looking at the Highwayman on the ground.

He knew that Aldora had shot the man through the heart and he had died instantly.

Samson had reared up at the two explosions, but the Highwayman's horse, as if too tired or too old even to be startled, merely moved away with his nose down looking for grass in the clearing.

As if what had happened was unreal, the Duke turned his head to look at Aldora who was a little way behind him.

The pistol was smoking in her hand, but her eyes as she stared down at the dead Highwayman were wide and frightened.

"Is . . is he . . dead?" she asked and her voice trembled.

"You saved my life," the Duke replied, "and the quicker we get out of here the better! You must not be connected in any way with this man's death."

"Y-yes . . of course," she agreed.

She put the pistol back into the pocket of her saddle from which she had taken it.

Then as if she realised for the first time he was injured, she exclaimed:

"His bullet hit you!"

The Duke looked down at his left arm and was aware as

he did so that it was already beginning to throb unpleasantly.

He could also feel the blood trickling down inside the sleeve of his coat.

With admirable composure he answered:

"The bullet will have to be extracted, and if we ride from here to my yacht, which is not more than two miles away in Bosham Harbour, I have somebody aboard who can remove it."

"Are you sure you can ride that far?" Aldora asked.

"I am all right."

Holding the reins in his right hand only, the Duke led the way back down the cart-track.

When they reached the road he put Samson into a trot, feeling that every movement shook his arm and intensified the flow of blood.

At the same time he knew it was imperative that they should reach the yacht as quickly as possible.

As if Aldora was aware of what he was feeling, she kept looking at him in a worried manner all the time they were riding in the direction of the sea, but she knew it would be a mistake to distract him.

She was aware that if as she suspected the bullet was lodged in the fleshy part of the arm he would lose a great deal of blood.

In fact, by the time they had ridden for a mile and the sea was just ahead of them she could see his left hand was crimson and the blood was dripping from it onto the side of his horse.

She, however, said nothing, and only as they drew near the harbour she allowed the Duke to ride ahead of her, knowing he would find his yacht quicker than she could.

When she saw it she felt it would be impossible that such a magnificent sea-going ship could belong to anybody but the Duke.

It certainly dwarfed all the other yachts in the harbour, and since it was tied up against the quay it was easy for them to approach it.

By this time the sun had come up over the horizon and turned everything, including the sea in front of them to gold.

As they drew their horses to a standstill beside the gangplank which had been let down from the yacht onto the quay, Aldora dismounted saying as she did so:

"Do not move. I will find somebody to help you."

Watching the Duke's face during the last part of their journey she was aware he was very pale and was in fact, on the verge of collapse.

She realised in the circumstances it would be very difficult for him to dismount without assistance, and it was impossible for her to help him and to hold both their horses at the same time.

She was wondering whether she dare leave her own horse loose when a sailor appeared on deck and she hailed him calling:

"His Grace is here and needs assistance! Fetch everybody available as quickly as you can!"

The sailor looked at her in surprise.

Then obviously recognising the Duke he hurried below and incredibly quickly three or four of the crew came hurrying down the gangplank.

Two of them ran to the heads of the horses and the Duke speaking for the first time, said in a weak voice:

"Tell Hanson to put the horses in my stable, then I want him to take a message back to where I am staying."

"Very good, Your Grace," the man to whom he was speaking replied.

Aldora having dismounted came to the side of the stallion.

"His Grace has been injured," she said. "Help him down as carefully as you can, then get him below."

She spoke with an authority which made them obey her.

Only as with their assistance he slipped to the ground did the Duke realise how unsteady he was, and it was with a superhuman effort that he managed to walk up the gangway.

As he moved he saw that the Captain had arrived on the deck and was reaching out his hand to assist him.

"I have been in the wars, Captain Barrett," the Duke said with an effort, "which means you will have to extract a bullet from my arm."

"The first thing is to get you below, Your Grace," the Captain replied.

As he spoke the Duke seemed to sag forward and he quickly put his arms around him and made a gesture to another man to support him on his other side.

By the time Aldora followed them, they had got the Duke below, and she wondered if she should assist the Captain or stay where she was.

Because she felt it might be embarrassing to be there while they undressed him, she walked into what she knew was the Saloon and thought it was one of the most attractive she had ever seen.

She was at first sight, extremely impressed with the Duke's yacht, and thought she might have expected that he would have a better, bigger, and certainly a much more up-to-date one than anybody else.

She knew quite a lot about yachts because her father had found it an escape from the endless social activities of his wife to sail away on his own to some quiet harbour where nobody could disturb him.

Because he adored his youngest daughter he often took her with him, and looking back after he was dead Aldora thought that the happiest times of her life had been when she was alone with her father.

They had been able to talk endlessly on the subjects which interested them both, but nobody else in the family.

She was admiring the pictures which had been executed by famous Marine artists when a man wearing the uniform of a steward came in through the door.

"Morning, M'Lady!" he said.

She saw he was a wiry-looking man getting on for middle-age, with a perky manner but a face that she felt she could trust.

"Good morning!" Aldora replied. "How is His Grace?"

"We've made 'im as comfortable as possible, M'Lady, and the Captain's getting ready to extract the bullet."

Almost as if Aldora had asked the question he went on:

"It's only in the fleshy part of His Grace's arm, thank God, but His Grace's already lost a lot of blood, and I expect he'll run a fever."

Aldora knew this was usual and she asked:

"I suppose you should find somebody to nurse him."

As the man looked at her she thought there was a twinkle in his eyes, before he replied:

"I be thinking, Your Ladyship, that you might be willing to do that!"

It had never crossed Aldora's mind for a moment that she would be expected to do such a thing, and she had been supposing that as soon as the Duke was comfortable she should return home.

Then she knew she could hardly leave him if she was needed, and what was more it would be the greatest mistake for anybody locally to know what had occurred.

They could all too easily connect the Duke's wound with the dead Highwayman.

Although it was very unlikely he would have to face a trial, there would undoubtedly be an enquiry which would result in a great deal of speculation.

What is more, explanations might have to be made as to why he had ridden away alone from where he was staying in the middle of the night.

If there was even a suspicion that he was, in fact, with a young woman, the inferences would be all too obvious.

Quickly, without even considering it further, she said:

"Of course I will help you nurse him, but I think it would be best if the Captain put to sea."

The man to whom she was speaking grinned.

"That's what His Grace said before I comes up to find you, M'Lady. He said no one's to know he's aboard, and Hanson, that's His Grace's groom, is to ride back to Berkhampton House and say His Grace has had a slight accident, but'll return in a day or two, as soon as he's feeling better."

Aldora could only admire the Duke for taking such a quick grasp of the unusual circumstances in which they found themselves, while he was obviously suffering considerably from his wound.

She considered whether she should send a message to her mother, then decided it would be a mistake until she had talked it over with him.

As she was thinking the steward said:

"Me name's Hobson, M'Lady, and I've been with His Grace for over ten years. I looks after him whenever he's ill, which's not often, but when a man has a fever and needs a soothing hand a woman's better at that than a man."

"I will certainly do my best," Aldora answered. Then she added:

"Before we put to sea will you ask somebody to bring on board the bundle which is attached to my saddle, and also everything they find in the pockets?"

"Of course, M'Lady!"

Hobson hurried away, and Aldora thought that, whether it was his own idea or on the Duke's instructions, they had made certain that she would not run off on her own as she had intended when she left home.

"It is my fault that the Duke has been wounded," she told herself, "and I must therefore do my best to make him well again."

Later when she went below to the Master Cabin, which was extremely well designed and more comfortable than any cabin she had imagined possible in a yacht, she saw the Duke.

The Captain had extracted the bullet, and now his arm

was bandaged and he was lying in bed with his eyes closed.

"I have given him something to make him sleep, M'Lady," the Captain explained, "and which will also make him forget the pain."

He paused before he said with a note of pride in his voice:

"His Grace bore it like a Trojan while I was removing the bullet. T'was a messy job, and he'll be as weak as a kitten for a day or two."

It seemed a funny way to describe the Duke who had always appeared to Aldora to be so dominating and overbearing.

Now as she looked at him, his face pale even in comparison to the pillows on which he lay, she thought he was like a fallen oak tree and no longer intimidating or, as she had felt, positively menacing, but instead rather pathetic.

"Did the bullet strike a bone?" she asked quickly.

"No," the Captain replied. "T'was just a flesh-wound, but it'll leave a nasty scar, and His Grace'll find it hard to use his left arm properly for some weeks."

"It might have been worse!" Aldora said, almost beneath her breath.

"What was His Grace a-doing, getting himself shot?" Hobson asked fiercely. "I've never before known him lose a duel."

"It was not a duel," Aldora replied.

"Not a duel?" Hobson repeated, his eyes alight with interest.

Because she was aware that the little man loved his master, Aldora told him the truth.

"His Grace was shot by a Highwayman who wanted to take Samson from him."

"A Highwayman!" Hobson ejaculated. "There's always riff-raff and vagabonds to be found tramping about the place when the races be on. But you'd think His Grace'd have more sense than to be a riding here through the night."

Aldora had no intention of explaining why the Duke was doing so and she said quickly:

"I think we ought to keep him as quiet as possible. Will you show me my cabin?"

Hobson led her into the cabin next to the Duke's, which was extremely well fitted out, and was very pretty with pink curtains over the port-holes and a pink bedspread over the large and very comfortable brass bed.

Everything else was set into the walls, the cupboards, the drawers, the dressing-table and the washing-stand.

The only movable furniture was a very solid armchair and a stool in front of the mirror where she could arrange her hair.

Because Hobson knew she was interested he took her round the rest of the yacht.

There were four large cabins for guests and two smaller ones with bunkbeds set against the wall.

"They be for lady's-maids or valets," Hobson explained. "Not that His Lordship's guests often bring their attendant with 'em. They're always more nuisance than they're worth!"

Aldora had heard this before and she gave a little laugh.

"Ladies get seasick and the Gentlemen grumble," Hobson went on. "As I says to His Grace a dozen times, them as likes the sea should be prepared to look after themselves."

"I am sure you are right," Aldora replied, "and I promise you, I am very good at looking after myself at sea."

"I might have guessed that, M'Lady," Hobson replied. "I knows if you're willing to look after His Grace you'd be able to look after yerself."

Aldora laughed again, then having taken off her riding-hat, and because the rising sun was very hot, her jacket, she went up on deck.

Already the yacht was out of harbour and they were in the open sea.

The sun was lifting the mist over the horizon, making a

golden haze of beauty which she wished she could show her father.

She had an idea that the Duke would appreciate it too, and she wondered how long he would feel ill and if he had been over-optimistic in informing her mother that he would be returning in a day or so.

"I wonder what excuses Mama will make for my absence?" Aldora asked.

Then she thought that nobody would miss her particularly while the fact that the Duke was not there to see his horses run would undoubtedly cause a great deal of comment.

She was quite certain her mother with her usual diplomacy would smooth over the surprise caused by his non-appearance, and it was extremely unlikely that anybody would imagine that because she was not to be seen they were together.

"When we get back and the Duke says he definitely has no intention of marrying me," she told herself, "he will return to London and there will be no reason for me ever to see him again."

At the same time, after she had been on deck for half-an-hour, and then came down to see how the Duke was, she felt guilty.

He was lying so quiet in the big bed and she thought it was entirely her fault that he was not at this moment looking forward with an eager anticipation of his horse winning the Goodwood Cup.

'I hope it does!' she thought.

She wished the Duke was awake so that she could discuss it with him and perhaps apologise for having run away at the wrong moment.

It had never struck her that he might follow her, and although she had acted on the impulse of the moment she had quite seriously intended to cross the Channel into France.

Then she would have disappeared until any suggestion

that she might marry the Duke was obliterated from her mother's mind.

She had brought with her a considerable amount of ready money, and also all the jewellery she possessed which was very valuable.

But despite the fact that she had been carrying a pistol with which to protect herself, she knew now that if she had been alone and had been held up by a Highwayman she might easily have been murdered.

Because she had always travelled either with her father or accompanied by a number of servants, Aldora had never really worked it out for herself how dangerous it could be for a woman on her own.

She had been so confident, because her father had taught her to be an excellent shot, that she need not be afraid of anybody or anything.

What had just happened in the wood had not only surprised but actually frightened her.

"I can look after myself," she had boasted to the Duke.

But now she was not so certain.

She could still see the Highwayman lying on the ground, and knew that while she had killed him to save the Duke's life, it would have been very different if he had been accompanied by another miscreant as dangerous as himself.

With all her brains and intelligence, Aldora was in many ways very innocent, and only as she sat down beside the Duke's bed did she feel suddenly afraid of the future she had chosen for herself.

She realised now that if at this moment she were travelling alone to France, she might be menaced by men who desired not only her money, but herself as a woman.

'I must have been mad to think I could manage on my own,' she thought, and was suddenly ashamed to think how stupid she had been.

It was much later in the day when Aldora was sitting

alone with the Duke that he began to be restless.

Hobson had already worked out some kind of rota for her and himself.

While she had luncheon in the Saloon he stayed at the Duke's bedside. Afterwards he had insisted that she rested and although she protested that it was unnecessary he replied:

"If His Grace's been up half the night, my guess is, Your Ladyship's done the same. Now you have a 'shut-eye', then you can watch over His Grace while I do all the things I've got to do, before I take over during the night."

"But that is not fair!" Aldora protested. "You will be doing much more than I will!"

Hobson grinned.

"I'm used to hard work, M'Lady, which is more than you are! I thinks it'll be better if you watch over His Grace during the daytime, while I watch while he sleeps."

"He may not sleep," Aldora argued, "and you have to rest sometime, so we will take turns both day and night."

She spoke so firmly that Hobson capitulated.

"Very good, M'Lady. You stay with His Grace until two o'clock, then I'll take over. How does that suit Yer Ladyship?"

"That sounds reasonable," Aldora replied.

Now Hobson had agreed that she should be with the Duke until dinnertime, after which he would get him ready for the night, and would make her up a comfortable bed on the sofa in the Master Cabin.

"I might fall asleep and not hear him," Aldora worried.

"You'll hear him," Hobson replied. "When you're on watch, the slightest sound rings like a bell in yer head, and it's instinct more than anything else that makes you aware that yer're wanted."

Aldora thought he was speaking of instinct almost in the same way as his master had done.

It was strange that nobody else, with the exception of her

father had ever discussed with her anything which was not entirely material and which one could see and touch.

She understood what Hobson was trying to say and let him have his own way.

Now as the Duke gave a little murmur and turned his head from side to side she rose from the sofa on which she had been lying and put her hand to his forehead.

As she suspected, his temperature was rising and she knew Hobson had been right in saying he would run a fever.

He did not however show any acute restlessness until about midnight when Aldora was dozing against the comfortable pillows which Hobson had arranged for her on the sofa while she was covered with a warm blanket.

Then she heard the Duke begin to speak.

Quickly she jumped up to go to his side, and when she touched him she realised that he was very hot and his skin was dry, in fact, burning.

First he began to murmur, then to speak. For a moment she could not understand what he was saying until his voice seemed to strengthen and he said:

"The - Russians! They - must be - stopped! Write to Sher Ali, ask - meet - discussions!"

There was a long pause. Then as he turned his head restlessly again and she was afraid he might move his arm he muttered:

"Keep the - Russians out of Afghanistan - important! Must be - done!"

She knew he was speaking as if he was already the Viceroy of India, and trying to repair the damage done by Lord Northbrook and the Gladstone Government.

She knew they had insulted Sher Ali so that he had accepted the Russian infiltration into Afghanistan.

Then as she realised the Duke's fever was rising she hurried to the small cabin where Hobson had told her he would sleep rather than in his own quarters so that he would be on call if she wanted him.

She knocked on the door and almost instantly she heard his voice say:

"I'll be with Your Ladyship in two secs!"

She ran back again to the Duke's cabin.

By the time Hobson joined her the Duke was talking incoherently, although she could recognise the words 'Russia' and 'Afghanistan' being repeated over and over again, and he was obviously running a very high fever.

"Don't you worry, M'Lady, we'll rub him down with vinegar," Hobson said reassuringly.

Aldora assisted him to lift the Duke up and put towels behind him.

Then when Hobson had mixed the vinegar with water, she helped him sponge his master down knowing that this was a very efficacious method of bringing down a high fever.

Strangely she did not feel in the least embarrassed at the Duke being half-naked.

In fact, as she worked him over dipping the sponge in the diluted vinegar, she felt he was like a child who needed her assistance and she longed to remove the heat from his body and the fever from his troubled mind.

They worked for over half-an-hour until the Duke's skin was less hot to the touch than it had been before, and although he still murmured incoherently his voice was much quieter.

"His Grace'll be better now," Hobson said.

He covered the Duke's chest with a fresh towel and left the sheet below his waist.

He then opened one of the port-holes to let in the cool of the night air.

She had been thinking so much about the Duke that Aldora had hardly realised that soon after dinner the yacht had let down its anchor and they were in calm waters.

She guessed, because it was what her father had always done, that the Captain had orders to let the crew sleep peacefully at night, and move only in the daytime.

There were so many small harbours and bays along the South Coast that she was aware that however rough the Channel might be there was always some place where they could heave-to and sleep undisturbed.

Hobson looked down at his master with a smile of satisfaction.

"His Grace'll be no more trouble tonight, M'Lady," he said. "Now you pop off to bed and don't worry about anything 'til the sun's high in the sky."

Aldora looked a little indecisive.

"You are quite sure you do not want some more sleep yourself?" she asked.

"I've had all I need," Hobson replied, "and unlike Your Ladyship, I don't have to worry about me beauty!"

He gave her an impertinent grin and Aldora laughed.

"Very well, Hobson. But call me if I am wanted, and I shall be very upset if you omit to do so."

"If yer asks me, His Grace'll sleep as quiet as a new-born babe!" Hobson replied.

"Then goodnight," Aldora said, "and . . . thank you."

She went to her own cabin, got into bed, and thought as she did so that she was in fact, very tired.

She had had no sleep the night before, and only and hour or so after luncheon.

Now she thought it might be impossible to sleep if she remembered all the dramatic events which had taken place, her escape from home, the thunderstorm, how she had killed a Highwayman, and the Duke lying in a delirium in the next cabin.

However she was so exhausted that she slipped away into an oblivion which was like sinking into a dark, comfortable cloud in which it was impossible to think.

The Duke, propped up against his pillows, looked at Aldora sitting beside his bed.

The sunshine coming in through the porthole lit her head

with a halo of gold, and he thought not for the first time, that she had a strange beauty that was different from that of any other woman he had ever seen.

It had a haunting quality about it which made a man look, and look again.

She was reading to him from a book of poetry which she had found in the Saloon, and he thought her voice was very soft and musical and had a kind of lilting quality in it that was unusual.

Aldora finished the poem and looking up said:

"I do not think anybody could describe a storm at sea better than that! Papa made me read whenever I felt seasick, and the words were so beautiful that I forgot about myself."

The Duke, because he had been thinking of Aldora rather than what she was reading, had not really listened, but now he said:

"One could hardly feel seasick with the sea as it is today."

"No, of course not," Aldora replied. "I wish you could come up on deck to see how beautiful it looks in the sunshine."

"I will get up tomorrow," the Duke replied.

Aldora gave a little cry.

"Only if you are quite certain that you will not hurt your arm or bring back the fever!"

She thought she had not convinced him and said:

"Do be sensible! Hobson and I sponged you until if I ever smell vinegar again I shall at once think of how worried we were about you."

"You can hardly expect me to apologise for something I could not help," the Duke remarked.

"I am not asking you to apologise," Aldora said, "only not to give us any more trouble, and Hobson is sure you should not think of returning to civilisation for at least another four or five days."

"Hobson clucks over me like an old hen!" the Duke

complained. "While you . . ."

He paused.

"Me?" Aldora asked.

"You have suddenly become a ministering angel: a role in which I never envisaged you when you were frightening me as a very aggressive Amazon!"

Aldora laughed.

"Did I really seem like that?"

"I was too intimidated to tell you the truth about yourself."

He did not wait for her to reply, but added:

"Now all is forgiven and forgotten, and I suppose you realise that after your saving my life I am not only eternally in your debt, but also your responsibility from now on!"

He spoke lightly, but he saw the colour come into Aldora's face and a wary look in her eye.

"What we have to decide," the Duke went on before she could speak, "is how I can reward you. You do not need money, and I imagine you already own a great number of jewels. I suppose therefore the only appropriate present would be a horse!"

Aldora laughed.

"You are very clever! It is not only something I would like above all things, but something I could quite conventionally accept."

There was a little pause before the Duke said in a different tone of voice:

"If you are talking about the conventions, Aldora, when my head ceases to feel as if it was stuffed with cotton-wool, which I suspect is due to some drug Hobson gave me after the bullet had been extracted from my arm, we have to think about you."

"About me?" Aldora enquired. "What about . . . me?"

There was not the hostile note in her voice that the Duke had expected, but an apprehensive one.

"Because you so kindly in your new role, came on the

yacht to nurse me, as Hobson tells me he asked you to do, you must be aware that if anybody heard of it, it would ruin your reputation!"

"I see no reason why anybody should know where I am," Aldora said quickly.

"I hope that is true," the Duke answered, . . . "but I am just wondering whether it would be wise to put you ashore somewhere along the coast of England and let you find your own way home from there. Or perhaps you have a better idea?"

Because it was the last thing she had expected him to say, she merely stared at him in astonishment before she replied:

"Are you suggesting that I should . . . ride back home . . . alone?"

"It would only be a question of finding you a horse somewhere near Plymouth," the Duke said in an impersonal tone, "and in fact my Captain knows a lot about horses. I have trusted him on several occasions in the past to bid for me at sales, in various parts of England which I have been unable for some reason to attend."

Aldora did not speak.

She was remembering what a shock it had been when the Highwayman had appeared so unexpectedly from the wood.

She could still see the man's face when he had been on the point of killing the Duke before she had shot him.

If she was riding home alone through unfamiliar country it would take her several days to reach Berkham House, and she knew she would find it extremely frightening.

As she did not speak, the Duke said after a moment:

"You must be aware that it would be impossible for me to send any of my crew with you because however carefully I briefed them they might inadvertently give away the fact that they were employed by me, which of course would mean our names would be associated, which is something you wish to avoid."

"Y-yes . . . of course," Aldora murmured.

"On the other hand," the Duke went on, "I suppose we could find a ship of some sort at Plymouth or Falmouth which would carry you back to Southampton. I imagine fishing-boats, if nothing else, make the trip regularly."

He frowned as if, while he spoke, he was thinking it out for himself.

"At the same time the boats would be filled with some very rough men, and I dare say not only would you find it uncongenial, but they might also insult you in one way or another."

Aldora felt herself tremble.

Again she was seeing the coarse, horrible face of the Highwayman.

After a moment, because she knew the Duke was waiting, she said in a faltering tone:

"M-must we make . . . decisions now? I would . . . rather wait until you are . . . well."

The Duke smiled.

"So would I," he agreed. "I like having you here. I like talking to you, Aldora. At the same time I have to think of what is best for you, and just as you have saved me from the Highwayman's bullet, I have to save you from the wagging tongues and the scandalous gossip of the Social World, who have never been taught to mind their own business!"

Aldora gave a little laugh.

"That is true! When I hear Mama's friends chatter, chatter, chatter about other people and – what they have said or done, I think what a terrible waste of time it is!"

"Indeed it is," the Duke agreed, "but I suppose all women want to 'chatter', as you call it, just as all men want a challenge. We want to fight a war, climb a mountain, or dig up some treasure that has been hidden for a thousand years!"

Aldora was listening obviously interested and he went on:

"But you are different from other women. What you want

is to discover the hidden teaching, the esoteric message written thousands of years ago, and understood only by a privileged few."

"Have you ever met any of those who did?" Aldora asked.

He knew there was an eagerness in her voice that had not been there before.

"I have met one or two men who I am certain had such hidden knowledge, although they did not communicate it to me."

"When did you meet them?"

"When I was in India."

"You did not tell me you had been to India!"

"You did not ask me!" the Duke answered. "Of course I have been to India. I was *Aide-de-Camp* some years ago to the Governor of Madras. It was an experience I shall never forget and I would have liked to stay much longer, but my father died and I had to go home immediately."

"And you have never been back?"

"There has not been an opportunity . . until now."

There was silence and he saw she was digesting what he had said.

Then, in the same indifferent tone of voice he had used before, he said:

"To get back to you, I think we must discuss how you can return home without having too many awkward questions asked as to where you have been and what you have done."

Aldora got to her feet.

"You are not to worry yourself about me," she said. "I want you to rest. You have the choice of shutting your eyes and trying to sleep, or else I will read to you."

"You are most regrettably like my Nanny, who always stopped me from doing anything I enjoyed because she thought it would upset me," the Duke complained.

"I can hardly believe you would enjoy planning what I should do," Aldora said.

"As a matter of fact I would," he answered. "You must

have realised by now that the one thing that really interests me is bringing order where there is disorder, or trying to attain perfection in something that belongs to me."

"Like Samson," Aldora said with a smile.

"Exactly!" he agreed. "Like Samson, my other horses and my estates."

He paused before he said:

"I would have liked to show you my house in Buckinghamshire, where I would defy you to find anything wrong that I am not already in the process of putting right."

"I would certainly try to find something," Aldora said, "just because I think you are too smugly pleased with yourself! Anyway, it has been too easy a task."

"Can you suggest a more difficult one?"

As he spoke his eyes met Aldora's and he knew they were both thinking of the task he had been offered with regard to India, which was so big, so impenetrable, that it would confound and terrify most men with its sheer complexity.

For a moment he held her eyes captive and it was impossible for her to move.

Then she said crossly:

"Will you rest and stop thinking? Just to make sure you do so I will read you something so incredibly boring that you will find sleep will be a welcome relief from it!"

"If you do that I shall throw my pillows at you," the Duke said, "and throwing them will be extremely bad for my arm!"

"Very well," Aldora conceded, "I will read you something soothing."

"You will find a book which I think will interest you on the bottom shelf of the bookcase in the corner."

Because for some reason she did not like to question she could not meet his eyes, she moved quickly to where she knew the bookcase had been built into the wall with the other furniture.

She crouched down to look at the bottom shelf.

There were a number of books on racing and three others which she knew were the ones he wanted her to find.

One was on Buddhism, one was entitled: *"India Today and Yesterday"*, and the third was called: *"The Secrets of Ancient India"*.

Almost despite herself Aldora's hand went out to draw the third one from the bookcase.

Even as she walked back to the bed she was aware that the Duke was lying low on his pillows, his eyes shut.

At the same time, there was a faint smile on his lips which made her suspect that he felt he had scored over her when she least expected it.

CHAPTER SIX

Aldora was drifting into a dreamland which seemed to merge with her thoughts.

She had before she went to bed, been thinking of how happy she had been during the day.

It had been exciting to be able to talk to the Duke without interference or without anybody thinking it strange that he should waste his time with anybody of so little importance.

She was well aware that the sophisticated Beauties with whom he amused himself would have laughed scornfully at the way they argued with each other on a dozen different topics as he lay in a deck-chair in the sunshine covered by a warm rug.

To Aldora it seemed very hot, but she was sensible enough to be aware that as he had lost so much blood, he would still be feeling cold on even the warmest day.

It was the first time the Duke had dressed and left his cabin, and as Hobson brought him a glass of champagne as soon as he was settled on deck, he said as he raised his glass:

"I certainly have something to celebrate!"

"That you are on your feet again?" Aldora asked, not quite certain what was in his mind.

"No, that I am alive," he replied, "thanks of course, to you."

She gave a little shudder.

"I do not want to . . . think about . . . it!"

"Of course not!" the Duke agreed. "But it will be something to put in your memoirs when you are old, and by that time you will doubtless have had a dozen other adventures to add to this one."

"I hope so," Aldora replied.

Then she changed the subject because she had the idea that if she went to India with him their adventures could really be worth writing about, while any she had at home would be banal.

Now as she recalled what they had said to each other during the day, she thought it strange that never once had there been a single word about India.

She had the feeling that the Duke had dismissed it from his mind and would no longer think about it, just as he would not think about a race he had lost.

"How could I possibly marry him when I dislike him so much?" she asked herself.

Then she suddenly knew that now she did not dislike him at all.

Her hatred had vanished from the moment he needed her ministrations to bring down his fever and she had watched over him at night.

She had risen whenever he had seemed restless to bring him a cool drink, and on several occasions when he was murmuring incoherently and twisting from side to side, she had massaged his forehead.

Then she found she could almost hypnotise him into going into a deep sleep.

Many years ago when she was quite small, one of her Governesses who suffered from extremely bad headaches had taught her how to soothe them away, and she was glad to be able to exercise that skill again.

Now as she was dreaming she was in India and talking to a Fakir who strangely enough looked like the Duke, she heard a bell ring.

Instantly she was awake, knowing it was the bell which Hobson had put beside the Duke's bed when he insisted that in future nobody was to watch over him at night.

"I am perfectly well," he said defiantly, "and although I

am very grateful to you, Aldora, and to Hobson, I am now able to look after myself."

Aldora thought what he said to be untrue, but knew it would be a mistake to argue with him.

Hobson however had other ideas.

"I'm going to put a bell by Your Grace's bedside," he said, "and if you feels in the night you want something, Her Ladyship'll hear if you rings it."

"I have no wish to disturb Her Ladyship," the Duke argued.

"All her's got to do is knock on my door, and I'll come to you," Hobson persisted.

"You are fussing over me again," the Duke said accusingly.

"And not without reason!" Hobson retorted. "If Your Grace does too much too soon you'll not be able to hold in them spirited horses. Then where'll you be?"

Because it was the sort of argument that Aldora felt she had heard from her Nanny, her Governesses, and at times her mother ever since she could remember, she laughed.

"It is no use," she said to the Duke. "Hobson will insist on having his own way! So if you do want anything, ring the bell and one of us will come to you."

The Duke had not said any more, but now, when she had been quite certain he would make every effort not to call them, she heard the bell.

Quickly she sat up and lit the candle by her bed.

Getting out of bed she put on a diaphanous white muslin wrap which was all she had been able to bring with her besides a nightgown and two very thin, light summer gowns.

She had not envisaged for one moment that she would not be in France within twenty-four hours and be able to buy everything she required there.

Now when she thought about it she realised it had been very improvident to ride away with so little and be prepared to spend the money she possessed on clothes, when she would doubtless have needed it to keep herself alive.

She was so confident that once she was in France she would be able to find a congenial place in which to lodge and some paid employment that she had not really considered the details of living on her own.

Now that she had time to think it over she was ashamed of being so foolish, just as she was ashamed of supposing she would not be in danger simply because she carried a pistol.

She was not in the least self-conscious as buttoning her wrap down the front she picked up the candle and hurried off to the Duke's cabin.

He was sitting up against his pillows, and as she stood in the doorway the candle in her hand she looked at him and realised he must be in pain.

She entered and shutting the door behind her asked:

"What is the matter?"

"My arm hurts, and I have a headache."

She went to his side and set down the candle.

"I was afraid you were doing too much on your first day," she said softly.

"Well, please either give me something to kill the pain," he said, "or massage my forehead as you did when I was running a fever."

Aldora looked surprised.

"I thought you were unconscious."

"I could hear your voice and feel you touching me," the Duke said, "and it was certainly very efficacious."

"Well, we will see if it will work now," Aldora replied, "but I think you should be flatter than you are at the moment."

Gently she took the pillow from behind him and when he was lower she sat down on the bed and leaning forward put her fingers flat on his forehead.

"Shut your eyes," she said quietly, "and think of pleasant things: of the sun setting in a blaze of glory, of the evening stars coming out one by one. The sky is growing darker, and yet at the same time more luminous."

Her voice was soft, low and almost hypnotic.

As she spoke she moved her fingers very gently over his forehead, soothing away the frown between his eyes which came from the pain he suffered.

"Now you are going to sleep," she said in a voice that was hardly above a whisper. "You are dreaming you are riding over the fields on *Samson* and you are happy, very, very happy, as you have everything you want in the world . ."

Her voice died away, and as she looked at the Duke in the candlelight she could see he was breathing rhythmically and his whole body was relaxed.

Very carefully in case she disturbed him she slipped off the bed.

Then as she took up the candle she looked back at him and said almost beneath her breath:

"God bless you, and the angels watch over you."

It was something her mother used to say to her when she was a child.

Once again she was thinking of the Duke as a small boy who had cried out to her because he was hurt and she had been able to help him.

She left the cabin.

Only after she shut the door behind her did the Duke open his eyes and lie for a long time looking into the darkness.

In the morning when Aldora was dressed she went to the Saloon for breakfast, and when she had finished she went out on deck.

They were now sailing Eastwards along the coast. She could recognise certain coves and bays they were passing, and knew that tomorrow they would be back in Chichester harbour.

That meant she would have to go home.

At least, she thought, the Duke had not persisted with his idea that he should put her ashore in Devonshire or Cornwall.

He had not spoken about it again and she had been afraid to ask any questions in case she did not like the answers.

The whole voyage had had a dream-like quality about it, but now she going back to reality and her mother would undoubtedly be very angry with her for running away.

At the same time she would be glad that she had returned and perhaps nobody else would realise what she had intended.

'Mama has only to say I was staying with friends,' she thought.

Then she felt her spirits drop and she felt depressed at the thought of the scene she would have to face when she reached Berkhampton House.

She was startled out of her reverie by the sound of someone coming out on the deck behind her and turning her head she saw with surprise that it was the Duke.

Hobson was with him, and while the Duke should have walked to the deck-chair that was waiting invitingly under an awning, he came to stand beside Aldora at the railing.

"How are you?" she asked.

"I had an excellent night."

"Your arm is not hurting you?"

"Hardly at all."

"That is splendid, but you must not do too much today."

"I have listened to all that from Hobson," the Duke said, "and I do not think I could bear any more!"

Aldora laughed.

"Now you are escaping from our clutches, but we are trying to hold onto you, just in case we have you back on our hands again."

"Would that be such a terrible thing to happen?"

"Of course it would!" Aldora said. "Think of all the things you should be doing, the horses you should be riding, the speeches you should be making!"

"Now you are frightening me!" the Duke exclaimed. "So I will definitely continue to rest for as long as possible!"

He walked away from her to sit in the deck-chair, lifting up his feet and even letting Hobson put a light rug over him.

While he was doing so Aldora thought she would change the book she had been reading and find another she could read to him when he got too tired to talking.

She knew there was nothing she enjoyed more than arguing with him and discussing subjects like strange countries, native customs, and world Politics in the way she had discussed them with her father.

Every hour she was able to be with the Duke she found more fascinating than the last.

Then when he looked tired she would insist on reading to him, and on several occasions when she had done so he had gone to sleep.

She now went below to his cabin because she had discovered that while there were books in the Saloon, all the ones that were most interesting were in his own cabin.

She was looking along the shelves, wondering what would be likely to stimulate their minds better than any of the others, when Hobson came into the cabin.

"I hope His Grace is not doing too much," she said, "and if he intends as seems likely, to return tomorrow, I think that is too soon."

"Yer Ladyship's right," Hobson said, "but His Grace has made up his mind, and you might as well try to drain the sea as get him to change it!"

There was silence as Aldora took out one book, then put it back again.

"If you asks me," Hobson went on, "a wound in his arm or not, the rest has done him good, and better than anything else has been his getting away from all them as battens on him in one way or 'nother."

He spoke violently, and as Aldora turned her face to look

up at him in surprise Hobson said:

"There's always gentlemen asking him for money, an' women as never leaves him alone, and they're the worst!"

Aldora felt this was not a conversation she should be having with the Duke's personal servant, and picking out two books from the case she stood up holding them in her arms.

"Your Ladyship's been the best thing that's happened to His Grace for a long time," Hobson went on as if he was following his own train of thought.

"What do you mean by that?" Aldora asked curiously.

"You've looked after him as if you were his mother, you've kept him amused an' not clung to him like a leech, which every other Lady he's had near him 'as done 'til I'm ready to believe they were trying to suck the life-blood out of him!"

Aldora looked at Hobson with surprise.

She knew because he loved the Duke and deeply resented his being imposed on, he was speaking with a sincerity that came from his heart.

"Surely they cannot be as bad as that?" Aldora asked.

"You don't know the half of it, M'Lady," Hobson said darkly, "an' they're at me day an' night to help 'em."

"To help them?" Aldora asked incredulously.

"It's: 'Dear Hobson, could you remind His Grace it's my birthday on Thursday?', and, 'Hobson, I must see him alone. Let me know when there's nobody with him.'!"

Hobson made a sound that was one of disgust before he said:

"But the worst ones are those who want me to tell His Grace how much they're suffering."

Aldora felt she should not be listening, but she did not want to walk away and seem unsympathetic.

"There was one of them," Hobson was ruminating, "who took the cake, she did! Lady Ludlow – no, Lady Lawson – that was her name! 'Tell His Grace,' she says to me, 'that

127

I'm going to kill myself, and when I'm dead he will be sorry!'"

Intent on what he was telling her Hobson did not realise that Aldora had stiffened as he spoke.

Then she said in a voice that did not sound like her own:

"I . . I cannot believe that any . . Lady would say that to you!"

"You'd be surprised what they do say!" Hobson answered. "That Lady Lawson sent me round the bend! As I says to her: 'Them as says they're going to kill themselves, M'Lady, never does!', and she didn't!"

"She must have . . been very . . unhappy!" Aldora said in a hesitating voice.

Hobson laughed derisively.

"Wallowing in her grief, that's what she was, until the next man came along! I sees her lady's-maid about a month ago and she tells me Her Ladyship's now threatening to kill herself over some Frenchy gentleman she took up with!"

Because she felt she could bear no more Aldora said quickly:

"I think His Grace is waiting for me," and hurried from the cabin.

She went along the corridor, but she did not immediately go out on deck.

Instead she stood in the Saloon, feeling that she must get her breath and adjust her mind to what she had just heard.

How could Lady Lawson have said such things to a servant, and the Duke's servant at that?

How could anybody who called herself a Lady be so vulgar as to discuss her love-affairs and her emotions with somebody who was not her equal?

It seemed inconceivable, and when she remembered how violently she had hated the Duke for inflicting such suffering, she thought for the first time that perhaps he was not as guilty as she had thought him to be.

With an effort she forced herself to go out on deck and sit

down in a chair beside him.

She put the books down and sat silent until the Duke asked:

"What is troubling you?"

"How do you know I am troubled?"

He smiled.

"Shall I say I am using my instinct? Or perhaps because we have been alone together for the last few days I have become aware of your vibrations."

"So you believe people send out . . vibrations like . . waves of . . light!" Aldora murmured.

"Of course," the Duke replied, "and your vibrations, may I say, Aldora, are very strong, very positive, but not as violent as they were when we first met."

He gave a short laugh before he said:

"The first night at dinner I could feel your hatred coming from you down the whole length of the dinner table, and I thought it was something I had never experienced before."

There was a little silence before Aldora said:

"Papa said that hatred was like a boomerang, and if you were not . . careful it . . swings back and hits the person who . . sent it out."

"Exactly!" the Duke agreed. "And I like to think, although I may be wrong, Aldora, that you do not hate me as actively as you did."

"I do not . . hate you at . . all!" Aldora replied, almost as if she was compelled to do so.

"Good!" the Duke said. "So when we leave each other tomorrow, it will be with feelings of good-will."

"T-Tomorrow?"

It was somehow hard to ask the question.

"What I have planned, and I feel sure you will think it is a sensible suggestion," the Duke said, "is that we will move into Chichester Harbour very early tomorrow morning, in fact at dawn."

Aldora was listening intently, but she also had the feeling

that she was holding her breath.

"Hamish, my groom, will bring your horse to the Quay, and he will also bring *Samson*."

"For you?" Aldora asked.

The Duke shook his head.

"No, that would be a mistake. You and Hamish will ride off immediately."

"I thought you did not like anybody riding *Samson* but yourself."

"Hamish has ridden him before, and you need have no worries that anything will happen on the journey."

Aldora was silent as the Duke continued:

"Hamish will leave *Samson* in your mother's stable and order my phaeton and team to come to the Harbour immediately so that I can drive back in comfort later in the day."

He paused before he said:

"Naturally we must avoid anybody at your house realising that you and I have ridden back together, so I suggest when you are half a mile from home you let him go ahead."

He paused before he continued:

"Then ride up alone in an undisturbed manner as if you had just returned from where you have been staying, with, a story that will convince your mother she need not have worried about you unnecessarily."

Aldora had the strange feeling that the Duke was settling her whole life for her, giving her no say in it, and he did not intend to listen to any arguments.

"I will arrive about five or six o'clock in the afternoon," he said, "and I will hope your mother will permit me to stay the night before I leave for London early next morning."

There was a long pause after the Duke had finished speaking.

Then Aldora said in what seemed even to her a very small voice:

"You . . seem to have it . . all planned . . out."

"Of course," he replied, "and I cannot believe you will be able to think of a better arrangement for us both."

"No . . no . . of course not!"

"Good!" he said. "We will therefore enjoy the sunshine, and as I suspect you wish to read the books you have brought out with you I will close my eyes and think happy thoughts that you believe are conducive to sleep."

He shut his eyes as he spoke and Aldora looking at him longed to ask him what he was thinking about.

Then she thought it would seem too personal and certainly too inquisitive.

He looked very handsome and, although he seemed somewhat thinner and certainly paler than before he had been wounded, she felt it added to rather than detracted from his good looks.

His eyes were closed, and she went on looking at him, thinking that perhaps never again would she have four days of being able to talk to a man in the same what that she had been talking to the Duke.

She knew her mother would have thought it thoroughly reprehensibly and doubtless the Dowagers who sat on the dais at Balls watching their daughters with the eye of a hawk would be scandalised.

What was more, the fact of her nursing the Duke, sponging him down when he was half-naked, and sleeping on the sofa in his cabin would mean that to protect her good name she would be forced to marry him immediately.

"Nobody must ever know," she told herself.

She knew the Duke was right in taking every precaution so that his absence from the races and hers could not be connected.

"Mama would force me to marry him," she told herself.

Then she began to wonder if that would be quite so horrifying as it had seemed when she learned that the Queen had suggested the Duke should marry her Goddaughter and take her to India with him.

When Aldora thought of India, it seemed like a golden enchanted land which contained not only the hidden knowledge that she sought, but also the happiness that she was somehow certain she would never find anywhere else.

It suddenly struck her that, although the Duke had told her he had been there, he had deliberately shut the door on her curiosity about the land that enthralled her, and this presumably was because she had refused to become his wife.

Now the sands of time were running out.

Tomorrow she would leave him, and it was only at parties and Balls that she was likely to see him again.

Even if he came to stay with her mother, which she thought unlikely, they would never be able to talk seriously or have any time alone together, as they had been able to do while he was in bed on the yacht.

'There is so much more I want to know,' Aldora thought wistfully.

She knew that above all things it was India that interested her most, but from which he seemed deliberately to have excluded her.

She thought now she had been very stupid, once they had come together again in the dirty Inn, in not pretending that after all she was considering what the Queen had suggested.

In which case he would have told her so much she wanted to learn before they finally parted.

Then she had the strange feeling that because the Duke was perceptive, or rather, as he said, he used his intuition, he would have known she was acting a lie and would despise her more than he did already.

As she thought of this it suddenly struck Aldora that she had been so busy hating the Duke that she had not questioned what his feelings might be about her.

He had made it very clear what he thought of her when she made a hideous face at him in the drive, and he had been extremely angry at her rudeness and the offensive manner in which she had spoken to him.

Then after she had saved his life and they were together on the yacht, he had been very different.

As she sat by his bedside reading or talking to him or even silent when he was half-asleep, she had felt there was a friendship between them which was different from anything she had ever known before.

He had relied on her, she thought, and knew it was because she was thinking of him as a small boy who had been hurt that it had been impossible to go on hating him.

Now, since her eyes had been opened by Hobson, she knew that what she now felt about him was very different from the condemnation and disgust she had felt ever since Lady Lawson had confided in her.

She felt as if suddenly she had grown up and was aware that the Beauty with tears streaming down her lovely face, crying out in anguish, was in fact unbalanced.

And, now that she could think about it dispassionately, she realised that Lady Lawson had gloried in her misery.

It was a situation Aldora had never encountered before in her life, and she had therefore been deeply moved by Lady Lawson's protestations of undying love and her repeated cries of how she wanted to die.

Aldora's brain told her now that Lady Lawson had been over-dramatic, over-emotional, and very, very unstable.

But at fifteen years of age she had felt, as she dramatically expressed it to herself, that 'her heart bled' for the unhappy Beauty, and her dislike for the Duke had grown as she thought of how much unhappiness he had caused.

Now once again she could hear the scorn in Hobson's voice and felt humiliated that she had been deceived into becoming over-emotional as the servant had been sensible enough not to be.

She looked again at the Duke and realised he was exactly like the hero in a novel, and it was understandable that women, even if they were married, should fall in love with him.

Who else of all the men, young, old, distinguished, who had come to Berkhampton House was so tall, so good-looking, and had such a presence about them?

This was due, Aldora knew now, not only to his rank and his wealth, but to a brain which would have been admired by her father and was, as the Queen had realised, exactly what was wanted in one of the most important positions in the world.

"He is unique!" Aldora told herself, and understood now what Hobson had meant when he said women would fasten on to him like leeches and it was almost impossible for him to avoid them.

They must have sat silent for over an hour before Hobson brought the Duke some nourishing broth which had been specially made by the Chef to strengthen him, and which he insisted he should drink.

"It'll do Your Grace good," Hobson said.

"I would rather have a glass of champagne!"

"Your Grace shall have that before luncheon," Hobson promised, taking away the empty cup which had contained the broth.

Aldora laughed.

"It is just like being back in the Nursery," she said, "and there is nothing you can do about it!"

"I am extremely grateful for his devotion, but just occasionally I would like to be allowed to decide a thing for myself," the Duke said.

"I expect if the truth was known, you would dislike it if you had to," Aldora said. "And do not forget that the ordinary, everyday comforts allow your brain to occupy itself with things on a higher plane altogether."

"Such as?"

"Horses of course," Aldora replied mockingly. "Politics, and your search for perfection."

"Which I suppose I shall never find," the Duke replied, "and why should I, when none of us are perfect?"

"You surprise me," Aldora teased. "I thought you were completely satisfied with yourself as you are!"

"I wish that were true," the Duke answered. "At the same time it would be a great mistake for any of us to achieve too quickly everything we wanted in life. We should look at the stars, and struggle towards them."

There was a little silence before Aldora said:

"What you are saying is that we only develop ourselves fully when whatever we are striving to attain is still out of reach."

"Of course," the Duke agreed, "and that is why a challenge is always a gift from the gods."

There was silence.

Aldora knew he was thinking of India and what a challenge it would have been, if he could have accepted the post as Viceroy.

She opened her mouth to speak, but as she did so Hobson came out on deck to tell them that luncheon was ready.

The Duke seemed rather sleepy during the rest of the day.

It was only when they dined together early, because he insisted that she had a long day ahead of her tomorrow, that they talked of some of the countries he had visited.

Aldora found herself absorbed in the history of the Arabs and the strange character of the Turks.

When dinner was over Hobson, who had been serving it with the help of two other stewards, said:

"Your Grace shouldn't be late to bed. You mustn't forget you've got a long drive ahead of you tomorrow, and doubtless Her Ladyship will have a party when you arrive, which you'll find tiring after having had only one person to talk to at a time."

He went from the cabin before the Duke could answer and Aldora laughed.

"I am sure you will miss Hobson when you go back to London."

"He will be coming back with me," the Duke replied.

"He is always with me, as a matter of fact."

He thought Aldora looked surprised and explained:

"I only sent him ahead to get everything ready for me on the yacht, as I intended to spend a few days on her when the races were over."

"Then Hobson is always with you."

"He is a terrible trial at times. At the same time I could not do without him," the Duke said simply.

"I can understand that, and I know he will prevent you from doing silly things that might hurt your arm."

"I wonder if he will be as clever at keeping me under control as you have been?" the Duke said reflectively.

As he spoke they heard the anchor being let down and knew that the yacht was in a sheltered cove where it would stay until just before dawn tomorrow morning.

"I suppose I should go to bed," he said. "As Hobson has said, I will have a long day tomorrow. So I hope, Aldora, you will understand if I say good-bye to you now rather than in the morning."

"Yes, of course," she said quickly.

"Hobson will call you and will see that you have everything you want, and you can trust Hamish to look after you until you are within sight of your home."

"Thank you."

The Duke smiled.

"You will of course both be armed, but they say lightning never strikes in the same place twice, and I cannot believe there are many such unpleasant Highwaymen lurking in the woods to accost you on your journey!"

"I hope not!"

"If you do have any adventures, I expect Hamish will tell me all about them. I doubt if we shall ever have a chance of talking to each other alone."

Aldora was sure this was true, and as the Duke rose to his feet a little carefully so as not to jar his arm she said:

"Shall I . . . ever see you . . . again?"

"I expect we shall bump into each other at parties or a Ball in London," the Duke replied, "but I suspect your mother will be annoyed with me so that I am not likely to be asked to stay again. Another year I shall be at Goodwood House."

Aldora did not speak and the Duke went on:

"I do hope there will be no unpleasant repercussions after our cruise, but if we are clever I am quite certain the secret of what really happened will be known only to ourselves."

He smiled at her before he repeated:

"Well, good-bye, Aldora, and thank you for saving my life. It was very clever and very brave of you, and something I shall always remember."

She looked up at him as he spoke.

Then, astonishingly, because she had not expected it, he put his arm around her and drew her close to him.

"I wish you every happiness in the future," he said softly.

He bent her head as he spoke and kissed her gently on the cheek.

Then when she thought he would kiss her in the foreign fashion again on the other side of her face, he pulled her closer still, and his lips were on hers.

It was a surprise, and yet as it seemed quite a natural thing for him to do in the circumstances, Aldora did not attempt to move away from him.

Her lips were very soft and innocent.

Then as she felt the hard pressure of his, she felt something strange and warm rise up inside her that was different from any sensation she had ever had before.

It seemed as if the sunshine had invaded her body and moved through her breasts until it reached her throat, and joined the Duke's lips with hers.

It was so exquisite, so different from anything she had known or imagined, and somehow a part of the music of the waves and the sunset that was golden in the sky outside.

Then before she could begin to savour or understand the

rapture of it, the Duke raised his head and she was free.

"Good-bye, Aldora," he said again, "and take care of yourself."

He walked away from her, opened the door of the cabin, and as she heard him going slowly and carefully down the companion-way she heard Hobson's voice, and knew he had been waiting for his master.

It was then she knew, incredibly and yet, if she was sensible, understandably, that she loved the Duke.

CHAPTER SEVEN

Driving away from the yacht, the Duke thought of all the extraordinary things which had happened to him since his arrival at Berkhampton House.

He realised, as he thought of it now, that he had not after riding so precipitately after Aldora, given Fenella Newbury a thought.

He supposed that if he had been polite he would have written to her at least to say how sorry he was that she had had to leave so unexpectedly.

Then he thought it was a good thing that he had refrained from putting anything down on paper whether intimate or not, and he had no wish to write secret *billets-doux* to Fenella or, for that matter, to any other woman.

He knew if he was honest that she was a closed chapter in his life and she had disappointed him as had so many other women before her.

What he was concerned with now was to make sure that the Marchioness was not over-curious about his injuries or where he had been to recover from them.

His arm was still a little sore and hurt if he moved it quickly.

But otherwise he felt well, although he knew that to drive his four horses himself would be too much of a strain.

As a rule the Duke disliked being driven, but his Head Groom was very experienced and competent and he found it quite a novelty to be able to sit back and enjoy the countryside rather than concentrate on his horses.

He had known as soon as the phaeton arrived at the

harbour that his plans had worked out as he intended and that Hamish had reached the stables at Berkhampton House, which meant that Aldora was also home.

He wondered what she would say to her mother, and if she would get into a great deal of trouble for having run away in such a ridiculous fashion.

He was aware that since she had been with him on the yacht she had understood what a foolish idea it had been of going to France alone.

The Highwayman had naturally been a considerable shock to her, as he had seen from her eyes, although he much admired the way she had kept her head and indeed saved his life.

Afterwards she had not moaned or continually talked about it, as any other woman would have done.

Because he was very astute and also, as he had said to Aldora, perceptive, he was aware too of how frightened she had been when he had suggested putting her ashore at Falmouth to ride home alone.

He could understand that because she was a good shot she had thought she could protect herself.

But he knew, although she had not said it aloud, that she wondered what would have happened if the Highwayman instead of being alone, had had another fellon with him.

"She has had to learn the hard way that life is not easy, and seldom what one expects," he told himself.

At the time he thought it would be a pity if she lost her confidence in herself and an innocence such as he had never known before.

He had never been with a woman who was so supremely unselfconscious, not only as it concerned him, which was surprising, but also never seeming, unlike the Beauties who were his usual companions, to think about her appearance.

With his experienced eye he had not missed the fact that she had with her only two gowns, both of them of very fine muslin, and she wore them in the daytime and in the evening without explanation or apology.

Because she used no cosmetics he could perceive the clarity of her skin and the natural colour of her lips, which with her up-turned eye-lashes made her seem very young and at times childlike.

At the same time when he called her into his cabin to massage the pain from his forehead, he had been aware that in her diaphanous nightgown and negligee which were almost transparent she was very much a woman.

Also with her golden hair hanging over her shoulders almost to her waist she looked very lovely.

She had not even then been aware of him as a man, and with a faint smile on his lips he thought it was certainly something which had never happened to him before and told himself it was doubtless a salutary lesson to his ego.

As they drove on, the sun was hot, and the Duke, although he was very comfortable and not exerting himself, knew he would be glad when they reached Berkhampton House.

As they turned in through the imposing gold-tipped gates, he wondered what sort of reception he would receive.

He was certain there would be congratulations, for he had learnt this morning when the newspapers were brought on board the yacht that his horse had won the Goodwood Cup.

Two of his other horses had also been easy winners on the last day of the races.

He knew in consequence that a large number of people would have noticed his absence.

But he felt sure that the Marchioness with her tact and her quick brain would have made some plausible explanation which everybody would accept.

All he had to consider now was the cause of his accident.

He had no intention of admitting to anybody that he had been shot at by a prowling Highwayman, and even to mention it might somehow connect him and Aldora with the man's death.

"I shall tell them," he decided, "that riding under some trees a low branch I had not noticed caught my head and caused me a slight concussion."

That seemed reasonable as it was something which often happened to riders out hunting or in the woods with which the countryside was covered.

As he proceeded down the drive the Duke was suddenly aware that his groom was slowing the horses and looking ahead he saw the reason for it.

Standing in the centre of the drive, as if what had happened at the beginning of last week was repeating itself, was a girl.

It was Aldora, and she stood waiting for the horses to come to a standstill, although this time there were no branches of wood to bar the way.

When finally the horses were halted she ran to the side of his carriage and looking up said to the Duke in a low voice:

"I must speak to you before you see Mama!"

"Yes, of course," he agreed.

He stepped down from the Phaeton and Aldora put out her hands to help him.

As he reached the ground the Duke said to his groom:

"Take the horses under a tree where they will be out of the sun."

"Very good, Your Grace!"

The groom turned the horses to the right across the grass and the Duke walked as he had before between two of the oak trees.

As he did so he was aware they were a little further down the drive than they had been on the previous occasion, and now there was a small copse of birch trees immediately ahead of them.

"I was thinking," Aldora said, "that it would be wise if we entered the wood. It would be a mistake for anybody to see us talking together, and then tell Mama."

They went a few steps further into the copse and found

inside a clearing where there was a fallen tree trunk on which they could sit if they wished to.

He stood however looking down at Aldora and waiting for he to explain why she wished to speak to him.

He noticed she was very differently dressed from how she had been on the yacht.

Her gown was an elaborate and very expensive one, and her hair, which she had worn twisted into a simple chignon at the back of her head, was now more skilfully arranged.

She looked indeed very lovely, but her eyes turned up to his were, he thought, apprehensive.

As she did not speak he asked:

"What has happened? Has anything gone wrong?"

"No .. nothing," Aldora replied quickly. "Mama was angry with me for running away, but she believed I have been staying with one of my old Governesses who lives near Chichester."

There was a little silence.

Then the Duke was aware that her fingers were entwined and because she was pressing them together the knuckles showed white.

"What is it?" he asked.

She looked away from him, her small straight nose silhouetted against the trunks of the birch trees.

"I .. I have something to .. say to you .."

"As you have already told me," the Duke replied, "and I am listening."

"I .. I was thinking as I .. rode home," Aldora said hesitatingly, "of what you .. said about a .. a man wanting a .. challenge."

"I remember that conversation, amongst many other interesting things we said to each other."

Aldora drew in her breath.

"I .. I know," she said in a voice he could hardly hear, "that it would be a great challenge for you .. and one you would enjoy .. if you were .. Viceroy of India."

She paused as if she was expecting the Duke to say something, but when he did not she still did not look at him, but went on hesitatingly:

"I therefore thought that . . because you are so . . clever and because I think you are undoubtedly . . needed in India . . at this moment . . I will . . if you still want me . . agree to come . . with you!"

The words seemed to be almost dragged from her lips as if it was a tremendous effort to say them.

When she had finished speaking it seemed as if everything was very quiet and even the birds did not move or sing as she waited for the Duke's reply.

It was a long time, she felt, before he answered in his deep voice:

"This is a surprise, Aldora! And are you thinking of me?"

"Of course I am thinking of you!" she said quickly. "And I know only somebody as intelligent as you could undo the harm done in Afghanistan by Lord Northbrook and the Gladstone Government."

"And you think that is more important than your feelings?"

"I . . I would . . like . . to go to India."

"Even though it involves going with me?"

She did not answer and after a moment the Duke said:

"I think you have forgotten something, Aldora, something very important."

She glanced at him quickly, then away again before she asked:

"What have I . . forgotten?"

"That your father said you should only marry for love."

The Duke spoke very slowly and quietly. Then as he watched the colour flood into Aldora's face he thought it was like the dawn moving into the sky, and just as beautiful.

There was silence, and after a moment, as Aldora still did not speak, he went on:

"Now that I know you so well, Aldora, I am convinced

that your father was right. It would be not only a mistake, but a crime for you to marry a man unless you loved him."

He was aware as he spoke that Aldora was trembling, and now he had the feeling that she wanted to run away and hide.

And yet she was unable to do so because she wanted to stay.

He did not move, but she felt that he had come nearer to her as he said:

"You told me that you no longer hated me, but I would be interested, Aldora, to know exactly what you do feel for me now."

He saw a little quiver go through her as he spoke. Then her eye-lashes flickered and her lips parted.

The Duke waited, not moving, until in a strangled voice he could hardly hear Aldora said:

"I . . I cannot . . tell you . ."

"Perhaps we could make it a little easier."

As he spoke he put his arms round her and drew her close to him.

She did not resist and in fact he was sure it was what she wanted, but was too embarrassed to say so.

Then as if he compelled her to look up at him she raised her head, their eyes met, and for a moment it was impossible to breathe.

Then slowly, very slowly, as if he savoured the moment and etched it on his memory, his lips came down on hers.

He was very gentle, and yet once again the softness, sweetness and innocence of her mouth aroused in him as it had last night, sensations he had never known before in all his many affairs with so many women.

He knew when he kissed Aldora that it was not only the first time a man had ever touched her, but also the first time she had felt the response of a woman towards a man.

It was as if her vibrations had joined with his and she had been swept into a strange world that bewildered and entranced her.

He had been aware for some time that to awaken her to the wonder and rapture of love would be the most exciting and thrilling thing he had ever done in his whole life.

All the time they had been together on the yacht he had found she intrigued and entranced him.

He had watched for her dimples, for the little specks of gold in her grey eyes, and the way, because he was so experienced, that she was opening out to him like a flower towards the sunshine.

She thrilled and excited him, and he had known that for the first time in his life he had to fight to win a woman and was far from certain if he would succeed.

Although he had been aware that her hatred for him was vanishing, he knew he could easily frighten her away by an unwary word or action.

Just as when in training a young horse he had to approach it subtly and very cautiously, so he had known that he must be careful of everything he said and did.

At the same time he had used all his intelligence in his campaign to capture her elusive heart.

It was something he had never done before, and when he had lain awake at night thinking of Aldora and what he would say to her the following day, he knew he was in love.

But in a way that was so different, so utterly alien to anything he had ever felt before, that at first he could hardly believe it was true.

Now, as he kissed her for the second time, he knew that while she excited him wildly as a woman, her clever mind stimulated his and they were linked together spiritually and mentally with a bond which would deepen and increase in the years ahead.

As he kissed her he knew that she was already his, even though she was hardly aware of it, and that he would fight to the death to keep her and would kill anybody who tried to take her from him.

To Aldora it was as if the gates of Heaven had opened again, and the ecstasy and rapture of the Duke's kiss lifted her up into the sky.

It was impossible to think of anything but the wonder of it.

Then as his lips became more insistent, more demanding, the sunshine she had felt moving through her body last night and which was there again became more intense until it changed from the golden glow of the sun into little flames that seemed to burn in her breast and on her lips.

It was as if they were ignited by the fire she sensed burning in him.

Only when she felt as if the glory of it was too overpowering and the Duke raised his head, did she make a little murmur and hid her face against his neck.

As he felt her whole body quivering against him and knew that she was shy, he thought it the the most perfect thing that had ever happened, and at the same time very exciting.

"Now tell me what you feel about me," he said and his voice was very deep and a little unsteady.

"I . . love you!" Aldora whispered. "I . . love you . . but perhaps you . . do not want my . . love."

The Duke's arms tightened.

"I want it more than I have ever wanted anything in my whole life."

The way he spoke was so surprising that Aldora looked up at him, her eyes very wide and questioning.

There was no need to put what she was asking into words.

"I love you, my precious!" the Duke said. "And I have been so desperately afraid that you would go on hating me, and I should lose you."

"How could I have been so . . foolish as to hate you? I love you . . but I never thought you would . . love me."

"It will take me a very long time to tell you how much."

Then he was kissing her again, kissing her until they were both breathless.

"How could I ever have guessed," the Duke asked when he could speak, "that anybody could make me feel like this? What have you done to me, my darling, and how can you be so different from anybody I have ever met before?"

He gave a little laugh, and before she could answer he went on:

"Of course we both know the answer. We have belonged to each other in previous lives, and perhaps when we reach India we shall find somebody to tell us about them, and learn for how long and how desperately we have searched to find each other."

"Do you . . really believe that?"

She saw the smile on his lips and pressed herself a little closer to him.

'I know it is true," she said, "but I am so . . humiliated and . . ashamed that I did not recognise you, when I . . first saw you, as the man who has always been in my . . dreams . ."

The Duke laughed.

"As I certainly did not recognise you," he said, "making that grotesque face and raging at me with all that hatred vibrating from you."

Aldora hid her face against him again and he heard her murmur:

"How can you . . love me when I . . behaved so badly and you . . might through my stupidity, have been killed!"

"But you saved me!" the Duke said. "Now, as I told you before, I am your responsibility. So how could you leave me to face all the dangers there will be in India without you to look after me?"

Aldora drew a deep breath.

"You are . . quite certain you really . . want me? Suppose, because I love you so much, that I . . bore you as all those . . other women have done?"

The Duke knew it was a very real fear, and he said quietly:

"Look at me, Aldora!"

She raised her eyes to his and he saw that while her lips were red and quivering from his kisses there was a touch of fear in the depths of her eyes.

"Listen to me, my precious," he said, "so that we shall never make a mistake over this again."

His eyes held hers captive as he went on:

"As you know, there have been a great number of women in my life, but all I felt for them was a very natural desire for their bodies."

Aldora made a movement which he recognised as being one of jealousy, but he continued:

"But while I find your face more beautiful, more alluring, altogether more captivating than any other woman's I have ever seen, you have something which they never had, and which is very much more important."

"What is . . that?"

"Your intuition, which makes it quite unnecessary for me to put into words what I want to say as we stimulate and inspire each other. I adore you and could never grow tired of your quick little brain, but there is still something more."

"More?" Aldora questions.

"It is difficult to find the right word for it," the Duke answered, "but I suppose it is what Christians call 'the soul', and the Buddhists think of as the spirit of life that is only temporarily enclosed in this body we use."

He saw by the shining light that came from Aldora's eyes that she was understanding what he was trying to say, and he went on:

"In that, as in our bodies and minds, we complement each other. We are one person, my darling, and even the ceremony of marriage will not make us closer than our Karma has made us at this moment."

Aldora gave a cry that was a note of sheer rapture.

"How can you say such things? How can you think in the way I have always wanted somebody to think?" she asked. "Oh, please . . love me . . and make me yours . . help me to understand as you do.. and teach me all the things I should know."

"That is exactly what I *will do*."

It was a vow.

Then he was kissing her again, kissing her until she knew that, as he had said, they were one person completely and absolutely.

What was known as 'The Bridal Suite' in the largest and newest P. & O. liner for India was filled with flowers.

There were so many flowers in the State Room that there hardly seemed room for any passengers, and the fragrance of the Madonna lilies in the bedroom scented the air.

Hobson began to move some of the baskets of exotic fruit from the chairs and tables on which they had been placed by the stewards, and to carry them outside into the corridor.

"They won't get through this lot until they reaches their Golden Wedding!" Aldora heard him muttering to himself.

She laughed, thinking she must remember to tell it later to her husband because she knew it would amuse him.

She went into the bedroom and began to take off the thin travelling cape which she had worn over the silk gown into which she had changed after the wedding.

It was the very pale blue of a summer sky and her bonnet was trimmed with tiny ostrich feathers in the same colour.

She put them down on a chair and knew that Hobson later would hang them up for her and would also unpack some of the large trunks which were already taking up too much room in the cabin.

She had agreed readily to the Duke's suggestion that she should not bring a lady's-maid with her from England but wait until she arrived in India.

There would be many experienced Indian servants to maid her in Calcutta, trained in their duties by previous Governor's wives or important Mem-Sahibs.

"English servants are always a nuisance in foreign

countries, and especially in India," the Duke said, "with of course the exception of Hobson. I could not manage without him!"

"Of course not!" Aldora agreed, "and he is very important to me too!"

The way she spoke made the Duke look at her curiously and she said:

"It was Hobson who made me . . understand how . . foolish I had been about . . Lady Lawson."

She did not look at the Duke as she spoke because she felt embarrassed.

And yet she wanted him to know that she no longer condemned him for what she now understood was not entirely his fault.

The Duke however put his arms around her and said:

"If there have ever been any other women in my life except you, I cannot remember them, and there is no point in your ever thinking about them."

She did not speak and he went on:

"I love you, Aldora! I love you more every moment we are together, every second that I think of you, and every time I touch you!"

She felt herself quiver at the passion in his voice as he asked impatiently:

"Why do we have to wait such a long time before we can get married? I find it intolerable!"

Aldora laughed and it was a very happy sound.

"Actually, darling, it is only three weeks," she said, "and I do not think any other Duchess or Vicereine has ever before been hurried up the aisle at such a gallop!"

"To me it seems like three centuries," the Duke groaned. "I want to be alone with you while, God knows, for all I see of you we might be living on separate Planets!"

"I know," Aldora agreed, "but Mama insists on my having a trousseau, although most of it will have to follow us later."

"I would be quite content for you to be with me in that very provocative nightgown you were wearing when you sat on my bed and massaged my forehead! It required all my will-power to prevent myself from pulling you into my arms!"

"I thought you had a .. headache and were .. in pain!" Aldora said reproachfully.

"A pain I hope never to suffer again, the pain of being unable to kiss you, to tell you how I was falling more and more madly in love with you!"

"How can I not have .. realised .. that?"

"I felt the only way I could win you was to make you think I was indifferent," the Duke explained, "although I was extremely anxious in case my plan did not work."

Aldora laughed.

"I think, darling, your plans will always work. You are so clever that I am prepared to believe you can do anything even as you have already taken the stars from the sky and given them into my arms!"

"That is what I will do when I really make you mine," the Duke said.

She thought now that he had spoken with a note in his voice that seemed to vibrate through her and even as she thought of him the door of the cabin opened and he came in.

He seemed to fill not only the small space in which they were standing, but the whole world, the sea and the sky.

Aldora's eyes as she looked at him were very revealing and the Duke shut the door and held out his arms.

She ran towards him and he pulled her close against him before he asked:

"Can it really be true that we are married and at last we can be alone together?"

"It is what .. I have been .. waiting for .. too," Aldora said and there was a throb in the words which told him how much it meant to her.

She had known when they knelt together in St. George's

Hanover Square and received the blessing of God that they were already joined by their belief in a faith that went back thousands of years before Christianity, and nothing, not even death would ever separate them.

But there was still a very human desire to be able to love each other completely and every night when she said her prayers. Aldora had prayed that the Duke would not be disappointed in her.

Now as he held her close and still closer she was a little apprehensive that she might fail him.

She thought he was about to kiss her again.

Instead he looked down at her and there was an expression of love in his eyes which seemed to transform his face.

"Once again we are at sea, my precious," he said, "and although this is not my own yacht, where there was only my own crew to look after us. I intend to enjoy my honeymoon by being alone with you and forgetting that anyone else even exists!"

Aldora looked up at him with a little smile waiting for him to explain, and as she did so she could feel the engines throbbing beneath them and knew the liner was putting out to sea.

Owing to the time of the tide they had not been able to cast off and sail until after dark.

Now there was hooting from the other ships and cheers from the Quayside as they moved away, but Aldora was not listening to them.

"What I have arranged," the Duke was saying and she knew he had planned out every detail, "is that our unpacking can wait until tomorrow. While we have a glass of wine in our State Room. Hobson will unpack just what we need for tonight. Then we can go to bed."

"I . . I would like that," Aldora said.

It had been a long, but exciting day and she had not slept very much the night before.

However she knew there was a far more important reason why the Duke wanted them to retire early.

She blushed at the thought and he smiled as kissed her.

They went into the State Room where there were pâté sandwiches waiting for them on the table and an opened bottle of champagne in which they could drink each other's health.

There had been so many people at the wedding for them to greet and shake hands with that the only two people who got nothing to drink. Aldora thought, and who hardly tasted the wedding-cake had been the bride and bridegroom.

The invitations had had to be sent out in great haste for everybody wanted not only to be present at the wedding of the Duke of Wydeminster, but also to say 'Good Luck!' and God Speed" to the next Viceroy.

The Prince of Wales had been a Guest of Honour at the wedding, as had the Prime Minister, Mr. Disraeli.

As the acceptances to the invitations came in Aldora said:

"I am beginning to understand how important you are and will be, and I am afraid that I shall be lost in the crowd!"

She was only teasing him, but there was a touch of seriousness in what she said.

"I am already making plans," the Duke had replied: "and as you know, I dislike my plans being disrupted, so that there will always be times when we can be alone together. I can assure you I shall insist on having my own way in this, if in nothing else!"

"You always get your own way," Aldora smiled, "and I am beginning to think it is very bad for you!"

"My way is your way," he replied. "I could say the same to you and predict that before my term of office is over you will be a very spoilt and very demanding young woman who expects the whole world to revolve around her!"

"Now you are being horrid to me again!" Aldora

complained. "You know that all I want to do is to make you happy and . . please you."

"You do please me," he answered, "but that is a very feeble word to express what you make me feel."

"I love you . . love you," Aldora whispered, "but I am so afraid . . I may make you . . angry at times."

The Duke smiled before he replied:

"I expect, my darling heart, that since we are both very positive and intelligent people, there will be many occasions when we will argue and even quarrel with each other."

"Oh! No!" Aldora cried.

"But," the Duke went on, "they will only be storms which will soon pass and be followed by a rainbow."

"Are you sure?"

"Very sure."

In the impulsive manner which always thrilled him she put her arms around his neck and said:

"Show me how to please you . . I am so . . ignorant about . . love."

"That is what I want you to be," the Duke replied, "if I ever find anybody else, except myself, teaching you I shall murder him, however much of a scandal it would cause!"

He spoke so violently that Aldora looked at him in surprise.

At the same time she felt a wild excitement because she was learning every minute they were together how much the Duke loved her.

She knew it was an overwhelming emotion that was as new to him as it was to her, and they vibrated towards each other until she felt at times even outsiders must be aware of the magnetism which flowed from their hearts and souls.

Then after Hobson had left them and the ship was moving under the stars down the English Channel, Aldora slipped into the large bed.

It was made up with the Duke's own monogrammed sheets and silk pillows trimmed with lace.

As she waited for her husband, she thought it was the reverse of what had happened before.

Then he had been in bed on his yacht and she had come to him.

There was only one small light beside the bed and it cast a golden glow on her hair and illuminated the lilies which stood in every corner of the cabin.

Only the Duke could have thought to make everything so beautiful for her. Aldora told herself, and as she thought of him he came in through the door which led from the State Room and closed it behind him.

He saw her waiting for him, her golden hair falling over her shoulders to her waist, her eyes wide and excited until they seemed to fill her whole face.

He sat down on the mattress facing her and took her hand in his.

"I love you, my darling," he said in his deep voice. "I seem to have fought a million battles to reach you, and stormed the gods to make sure you would be mine!"

'I . . I am yours!" Aldora said softly.

The Duke looked into her eyes for a long moment.

Then he kissed her hands, first one then the other, before he got into bed beside her.

He put his arms around her, and felt her quivering against him, not with fear, but with the same wild excitement he felt rising within himself.

He knew the sensations she aroused were so glorious, so wonderful that it was the perfection he had thought he would never find.

He drew her closer as he said:

"I worship you, my darling, and because I have so much to teach you you must help me to be very gentle and not frighten you in any way."

"I am . . not frightened . . I could never be . . frightened with you," Aldora said. "In fact I know now that . . love casts out fear . . hatred . . and . . wrong."

It was almost as if she asked him the question and he answered:

"I believe that too and, darling, what I want to give you now that we are together is the beauty which we shall find in India."

She made a little murmur of joy and went on:

"It is the love which will carry us through all the difficulties and problems, and reveal to us the secrets which you have been seeking for so long."

"I am sure those secrets are already in our souls Aldora replied, and when our minds discover them, we shall learn that they are each one of them . . motivated by . . love."

The Duke thought this was something they would discuss and argue over in the future, and it would absorb them both.

Then because Aldora was so close to him that he could feel her heart beating, the fire was rising within him and his lips were aching to kiss her.

He kissed her eyes, her straight little nose, then her mouth.

As he moved lower to kiss the softness of her neck he knew that he aroused in her new sensations she had never known before and which complemented those which consumed him.

The vibrations that came from them both were filled with the light which came from the stars, the light of their enquiring minds, and the light of love.

As it emanated from them, covered them, and dazzled their eyes they were lifted up on the peaks of ecstasy.

Then as the Duke made Aldora his they were one with the gods.

THE END

BARBARA CARTLAND TITLES
AVAILABLE FROM CORGI BOOKS

WHILE EVERY EFFORT IS MADE TO KEEP PRICES LOW, IT IS SOMETIMES NECESSARY TO INCREASE PRICES AT SHORT NOTICE. CORGI BOOKS RESERVE THE RIGHT TO SHOW AND CHARGE NEW RETAIL PRICES ON COVERS WHICH MAY DIFFER FROM THOSE ADVERTISED IN THE TEXT OR ELSEWHERE.

THE PRICES SHOWN BELOW WERE CORRECT AT THE TIME OF GOING TO PRESS (JUNE '85).

☐	12443 5	A REBEL PRINCESS	£1.50
☐	12442 7	THE UNBREAKABLE SPELL	£1.50
☐	12441 9	THE SCOTS NEVER FORGET	£1.50
☐	12397 8	JOURNEY TO A STAR	£1.25
☐	12373 0	THE DUKE COMES HOME	£1.25
☐	12349 8	LIGHT OF THE GODS	£1.25
☐	12208 4	WISH FOR LOVE	£1.00
☐	12247 5	MISSION TO MONTE CARLO	£1.00
☐	12168 1	THE POOR GOVERNESS	£1.00
☐	11787 0	DOLLARS FOR THE DUKE	95p
☐	11840 0	WINGED MAGIC	95p
☐	10169 9	NEVER LAUGH AT LOVE	95p
☐	10168 0	A DREAM FROM THE NIGHT	95p
☐	10228 8	THE SECRET OF THE GLEN	95p
☐	11876 1	A PORTRAIT OF LOVE	95p
☐	10229 6	THE PROUD PRINCESS	95p
☐	10255 5	HUNGRY FOR LOVE	95p
☐	10745 X	LOVE AND THE LOATHSOME LEOPARD	95p
☐	10786 7	NO ESCAPE FROM LOVE	95p
☐	10305 5	THE DISGRACEFUL DUKE	95p
☐	10602 X	PUNISHMENT OF A VIXEN	95p
☐	11930 X	A SHAFT OF SUNLIGHT	95p
☐	10549 X	A DUEL WITH DESTINY	95p
☐	11136 8	WHO CAN DENY LOVE	95p
☐	10690 9	THE LOVE PIRATE	95p
☐	10744 1	A TOUCH OF LOVE	95p
☐	11045 0	LOVE CLIMBS IN	95p
☐	11097 3	A NIGHTINGALE SANG	95p
☐	10803 0	THE SAINT AND THE SINNER	95p
☐	10903 7	LORD RAVENSCARS REVENGE	95p
☐	10902 9	THE CHIEFTAIN WITHOUT A HEART	95p
☐	10946 0	THE RACE FOR LOVE	95p
☐	10994 0	THE DUKE AND THE PREACHER'S DAUGHTER	95p
☐	11027 2	LOVE IN THE CLOUDS	95p
☐	12009 X	FOR ALL ETERNITY	£1.00
☐	10804 9	THE PROBLEM OF LOVE	95p
☐	12068 5	SECRET HARBOUR	£1.00
☐	12085 5	THE VIBRATIONS OF LOVE	£1.00

All these books are available at your bookshop or newsagent, or can be ordered direct from the publisher. Just tick the titles you want and fill in the form below.

CORGI BOOKS, Cash Sales Department, P.O Box 11, Falmouth, Cornwall.

Please send cheque or postal order, no currency.

Please allow cost of book(s) plus the following for postage and packing:

U.K. Customers – Allow 55p for the first book, 22p for the second book and 14p for each additional book ordered, to a maximum charge of £1.75.

B.F.P.O. and Eire – Allow 55p for the first book, 22p for the second book plus 14p per copy for the next seven books, thereafter 8p per book.

Overseas Customers – Allow £1.00 for the first book and 25p per copy for each additional book.

NAME (Block Letters) ....

ADDRESS ....

....